Seeking Fortune Elsewhere

Stories

Sindya Bhanoo

This is a work of fiction. All of the characters, organizations, and events portrayed in this novel are either products of the author's imagination or are used fictitiously.

Grateful acknowledgment is made to the following journals where some of these stories first appeared:
"Malliga Homes" and "Amma" in *Granta*; "His Holiness" in *American Literary Review*; "No. 16 Model House Road" in *New England Review*; "A Life in America" was published as "Different" in *Masters Review*; "Three Trips" was published as "Nothing Like Ice Cream" in *Glimmer Train*

Hardcover ISBN: 978-1-64622-087-8
Paperback ISBN: 978-1-64622-173-8

Cover design and illustration by Dana Li
Cover photograph © iStockphoto.com / ilotyna
Book design by Wah-Ming Chang

Library of Congress Control Number: 2021937441

Catapult
New York, NY
books.catapult.co

Printed in the United States of America
1 3 5 7 9 10 8 6 4 2

a sense of diaspora and displacement. But one can't help but feel that in her brilliant writing, Bhanoo has found her place."

—Valerie Wu, *Asia Pacific Arts*

"As a collection, *Seeking Fortune Elsewhere* achieves a level of poignancy most writers can only dream of . . . We see just how complex the immigrant experience can be and how asserting one's individuality can grant characters a way out of the past—or lead them back to it."

—Rajpreet Heir, *Harvard Review*

"Each of the stories creates a new world for us to inhabit ... and the cumulative effect is rich and layered, an intimate look into these characters' lives. It is rare for all the stories in a collection to feel equally realized, but this collection manages to do just that."

—Laura Spence-Ash, *Colorado Review*

"Bhanoo's brilliance is in her ability to transform stories of individuals from specific poignance to universal experience."

—*The Adroit Journal*

"Bhanoo's prose is delicate, spare, and radiant with emotion . . . *Seeking Fortune Elsewhere* is a companion in healing, a book that surfaces our longing and vulnerability."

—Melody S. Gee, *Commonweal*

"Bhanoo captures both the tenacity and tender humanity of her protagonists."

—Supriya Saxena, *Zyzzyva*

"Sindya Bhanoo describes her characters with an astonishing mixture of mercy and mercilessness, which is to say they live and breathe and will break your heart and stun you."

—Elizabeth McCracken, author of *The Souvenir Museum*

"How thrilling to see women I know in these pages, tender and fierce, yearning for freedom yet plagued by the past. Every one of these stories glows with truth."

—Tania James, author of *The Tusk That Did the Damage*

"This achingly beautiful collection charts the emotional journeys and complicated ties of those who choose to leave and those who are left behind. A magnificent debut of a writer you will read for years to come."

—Lara Prescott, author of *The Secrets We Kept*

"*Seeking Fortune Elsewhere* is a rare and breathtaking achievement . . . With her boundless talent, fierce intellect, and abiding curiosity about the souls of her characters, Sindya Bhanoo arrives as one of the most important writers of her generation."

—Bret Anthony Johnston, author of *Remember Me Like This*

"With wise, honest precision and compassionate grace, Sindya Bhanoo masterfully locates the tender sources of human longing. *Seeking Fortune Elsewhere* is a stunning collection by an extraordinary talent."

—Jill McCorkle, author of *Hieroglyphics*

Praise for *Seeking Fortune Elsewhere*

Winner of the 2022 New American Voices Award
Long-listed for the 2023 Andrew Carnegie Medal for Excellence

"The stories in Sindya Bhanoo's *Seeking Fortune Elsewhere* are both fierce and tender, suffused with longing but also unsparing in their exploration of the dynamics among family members, loved ones, and cultures. Bhanoo is an immensely talented writer who packs deep emotional punches into stories told economically and with elegant restraint."

—Christopher Castellani, judge for the Institute for Immigration Research New American Voices Award

"Tender and precise . . . Bhanoo's focus is clear and tightly observed, centering the decisions and difficulties of a global life, some of them gut-wrenching . . . These stories rattle and shake with the heartache of separation, rendering palpable the magnitude of small decisions in our less-than-small world."

—Samantha Hunt, *The New York Times Book Review*

"An extraordinary debut collection centering the complex and diverse experiences of South Asian immigrants."

—Karla J. Strand, *Ms.*

"Exquisite . . . Bhanoo's piercing stories further augment the growing shelves of spectacular first short story collections by women of color."

—*Booklist* (starred review)

"Bhanoo transforms human drama into mystery. Graceful stories by a writer with enormous empathy for even the most flawed and forlorn among us." —*Kirkus Reviews* (starred review)

"Stunning . . . Bhanoo finds novel ways for her protagonists to cope with adversity . . . This introduces a great new talent."
—*Publishers Weekly* (starred review)

"With *Seeking Fortune Elsewhere* and its glimpse into the lives of Tamil immigrants, Bhanoo artfully extends the burgeoning South Asian American literary canon's trajectory."
—Meena Venkataramanan, *Pittsburgh Post-Gazette*

"Yearning drives the characters in Sindya Bhanoo's elegant, sensitive debut collection *Seeking Fortune Elsewhere* . . . Bhanoo makes the reader feel every heartbreak through her skillful, measured prose." —Jenny Shank, *Star Tribune*

"Written with a roving curiosity, Bhanoo's characters live and breathe like real people, their paths branching off the page and twining into your heart." —*Chicago Review of Books*

"The appeal of *Seeking Fortune Elsewhere* resides in its gentle trust that culturally faithful stories can and should slip easily across borders." —Anita Felicelli, *Alta*

"Bhanoo's command of language is meditative and deeply human . . . *Seeking Fortune Elsewhere* may be ingrained in

For my parents,
Udaya and C. R. Narayanaswamy,
who went elsewhere

"Do you understand the sadness of geography?"

—Michael Ondaatje, *The English Patient*

Contents

Seeking Fortune Elsewhere

Malliga Homes

Winner of the O. Henry Prize

Mr. Swaminathan died as he was walking back to his flat from the Veg dining hall after dinner. He was ahead of me on the path, and I saw him slow down. His gait changed from a fast stride to a slower, hunched walk. His left arm went limp. He lost his footing and crumpled to the ground. If I had not been swift, I imagine, he would have hit his head on the concrete. There would have been blood. But I caught up with him. Before he fell, I squatted to the ground and put my hands out, and his head fell directly into my open palms. Carefully, I slipped my hands out, set his head gently on the concrete, and sat at his side talking to him. His left eye looked lower than his right. His left cheek sagged, as if it might slide off.

I held his hand until the ambulance arrived. It was the first time that I had held a man's hand since my husband died. The rectangular diamond on Mr. Swaminathan's gold ring was hard and cold in contrast to his warm skin. Before they loaded his body onto the gurney, he opened his eyes, looked at me, and said, "Renuka." Then he squeezed my hand. Whether he was asking me to summon his wife, or whether he thought I *was* his wife, I cannot say. He died before he reached the hospital. He was seventy-five years old, the same age my husband would be if he were alive today.

His death was our first. Hard to believe, since this is a place for old people. But Malliga Homes is a new facility, and the first residents, myself included, moved in just two years ago.

The other day, I spoke to my daughter, Kamala, on the phone, and told her how expertly the personnel handled the whole Swaminathan matter. They were prompt in calling for help. The area was cleared immediately, and the ambulance rolled right onto the freshly trimmed landscaping, crushing a row of golden dewdrop shrubs that took a year to grow.

"I am so glad to hear that," Kamala said.

Malliga Homes is not a bad place. It is a rather nice place, in fact. Just a bit isolated for city people like me, coming from places like Chennai and Bangalore. The facility sits at the intersection of Thambur Road and NH-181, just outside of Coimbatore. Going to the outskirts of a mid-sized city gave the developers more space, and allowed them to invest in luxuries that we all appreciate. We have stone tiles in the bathrooms, Thermofoil cabinets, those wood laminate floors that are in style now, picturesque landscaping, and Honda inverter generators with eight hours of run time for when the power goes out, which it does daily.

I am lucky to be here, my Kamala likes to remind me. It is only the second place of its kind in South India, and the units sold out quickly. Still, no amount of expensive stone or carefully worded praise from my daughter can change what Malliga Homes is: a place for those who have nowhere else to go.

We are of the upper middle class, here. We do not come from families who own hospitals or factories, or vast tracts of land. We work for those people—*worked* for those people. Those people belong to a different cut entirely, and will never move here, no matter how beautifully our gardeners maintain the bougainvillea vines and the oleander shrubs. Those people will stay in their posh city flats with their many servants, with their children nearby. The offspring of the rich are rich, and they do not seek their fortunes elsewhere.

Like me, nearly every resident of Malliga Homes has lost sons and daughters to Foreign. That is the reason we live in a retirement-community-cum-old-age-home, rather than with our families. My Kamala left India twenty-five years ago. She is deputy managing director of a company called Synchros Systems, in the Atlanta area.

Renuka Swaminathan also has two children living abroad, one in Germany and one in Australia. They must have arrived already, to help with Mr. Swaminathan's kariyam preparations.

I am knitting a sweater made of fine green mohair for Renuka. After the kariyam, she is going to Adelaide to spend time with her son. I was the one who said, "Better to go. It is depressing to be alone right after." Her son is the manager of a movie theater there. He was not able to finish his graduate degree at the University of Adelaide, but somehow found a way to stay in the country. "Good for him," I said, when Renuka told me. I meant it.

Those of us at Malliga Homes with children in America rank higher than those with children in Dubai or Qatar. Somewhere in between fall those with children working in Singapore, Australia, England, Germany, and the rest of Western Europe. Africa falls below the Middle East, both because of what people imagine it is like there, and because it is so hard to get to. What our children do, how much money they make, whether our grandchildren are bright or mediocre—all of this matters. It is a tragedy to have a brilliant child and a dunce of a grandchild.

The yarn for Renuka's sweater cost me four rupees per gram, much more than I typically pay, but I decided it was worth it. The sweater will bring out the green in her eyes and it will be good for the Australian winter. I checked the climate in Adelaide on the Net; it can drop down to ten degrees. But also: Death turns you cold, and I want Renuka to stay warm. In the months after my husband died, a chilliness plagued my being, even in hot weather.

My husband's death was what brought me to Malliga Homes. After he died, Kamala flew to India and spent two weeks with me in our Chennai flat. She insisted that I leave my red bottu on my forehead, and keep all my jewelry on.

"This is not the end of life for you, Amma. I don't believe in such things," she said.

I did insist on taking off my toe rings. I never liked them. Initially, they would not come off; Kamala tried to help, and gave up. They had been on for forty-five years, the silver rings tightening around my toes as I became fatter over the decades, my flesh curling over their edges. Finally, after soaking my feet in soapy water for thirty minutes, I had success.

Kamala collapsed on our cane sofa, the same one she spent years reading on as a teenager, her legs leisurely stretched out while she held Somerset Maugham high above her head. Her eye makeup was smeared from crying. Both of us had done a lot of that.

"Amma, come lie down with me," she said, a cricket ball in one hand and a brochure in the other. My husband loved cricket, and she had been carrying the ball around with her since her arrival.

"Move," I said.

We lay squished on the sofa, side by side, hip to hip, mother and daughter. She handed me a brochure.

"It's called Malliga Homes," she said. "Look how nice the grounds are. Like Brindavan Gardens."

The brochure was from Kamala's friend in America, Padmini Venugopal. Padmini's parents had just moved into Malliga Homes.

"'All the comforts of home, without any worry—and so many friends,'" Kamala read out loud. She looked at me eagerly.

"Consider it," she said.

"What friends?"

"You will make them."

"Are you telling me what to do? What if I had stopped you all those years ago from going to America alone?" I asked.

"This is not the same thing," she said. She sat up and climbed over me to get off the sofa. "It is not the same thing at all."

The following night, I had a small fall in the bathroom. Though I was not seriously injured, Kamala became unstoppable. I could hear the determination in her voice, like when she was a girl and wanted a peach Melba from Jaffar's on Mount Road. She would not stop until I relented.

"You are my responsibility now," she said. She was combing my hair, because I sprained my right wrist in the fall and could not do it myself. "I've already made a booking. I paid the deposit today."

After she tied my white hair into a loose bun, she stroked my head as if I were a child. Her own hair, long and braided, was speckled with white.

"It's a two-bedroom," she said. "So we can visit you."

She extended her trip by a week, so that she could move me into Malliga Homes.

Two years have passed and they have not visited. They were all supposed to be here this time next month—Kamala, my son-in-law, Arun, and my granddaughter, Veena. I prepared the bedroom for them as soon as Kamala told me the plan. I bought new sheets and an extra single bed. But just a few weeks ago, Kamala called to say she was coming alone. Arun is busy with work. Veena started a new job.

They would enjoy it here. It is like a resort. There are two swimming pools on the property, and a boy scoops out the leaves with his large net many times each day. The Veg and Non-Veg food is cooked in separate kitchens. We have tennis matches, movies in Tamil, Hindi, and English on the big screen in the lounge, yoga, a walking group, a bridge group, and a Hindu prayer group that meets at the small temple we built within the compound. There are smaller Muslim and Christian prayer groups that meet in residents' homes. Malliga Homes, as Kamala says, is "inclusive."

There is nothing wrong with Alpharetta, Georgia, where Kamala lives, but for all the space and privacy that America offers, it is a country that longs for life. You go for a drive and the road is endless. One fast food restaurant after another. Wendy's. McDonald's. Waffle House. The colored lights shine bright in the evenings, beckoning visitors. "Like temples," I used to say. The grocery store is three kilometers from their house. What sort of place is that? One where people are too busy driving to enjoy life, I suppose. Nobody has time to talk, and yet everyone is seeing a therapist.

"It is only a ten-minute drive to Starbucks," Kamala would say, when we visited. "Should we go?"

Ten minutes. I may as well plant a tree, pluck the beans myself, and grind my own coffee, I often said to my husband. He would gently put his palm over my hand and whisper, "Shush. She may hear you."

He spoiled her. The best school. The best tutors. The clothes she wanted. The books she liked. Let her go to the movies. Let her relax. *No need to make her cook with you*, he would say. *Do not trouble her. Do not upset her. Let her be.*

He was just as bored as I was in Alpharetta, even if he never said so. He, too, hated the burned taste of Starbucks, and how we went the whole day in America—the whole bloody day—without seeing a single person but the mailman, while Kamala and Arun went to work and Veena went to school. I always enjoyed living right in the heart of Chennai, with the noises of the street cluttering my day. Everything I needed was a stone's throw away.

"No point in living in the city in America," Kamala said, back when they bought the house. "Dirty, unsafe, no parking, bad schools." She said "America," but was she also talking about her childhood home? I could not help but wonder.

What do you do with a big, empty house, full of rooms that you do not need? She never talks about this, but somewhere inside of her she must feel it. She is my daughter after all. Her house, with its vaulted ceilings and skylights, it was no better than Malliga Homes.

At least she is in America. All those years ago, when her Georgia Tech admissions letter arrived, I said this to my husband.

"If she has to go, let it be there."

I dine with the Venugopals, the parents of Kamala's friend Padmini. Over his empty plate, as we wait to be served, Dr. Venugopal cannot stop talking about Mr. Swaminathan's death.

"For me, it is an intellectual curiosity," he says. He is a retired cardiologist. His wife, Lakshmi, fit and elegant, has gray hair but smooth skin, undoubtedly from years of sandalwood paste facials. We are in the Non-Veg dining hall, and Mr. and Mrs. Sharma are also with us. The Venugopals and the Sharmas always sit together. Only once before have I been invited to join them, when I first moved in. It was a sort of welcome and thank-you. When Kamala signed me up for Malliga Homes, the Venugopals received something called a "referral bonus," by way of a free out-of-station trip to Ooty.

The Sharmas and the Venugopals are sipping gin and tonics. Dr. Venugopal summons the mobile bartender with his fully stocked cart for me. I order a fresh lime soda. Alcoholic drinks cost extra, and I do not like to waste money.

After listening to me describe the way Mr. Swaminathan fell, how his face drooped on one side, how his speech slurred as he said his wife's name, Dr. Venugopal declares that it was most certainly an ischemic stroke, not a hemorrhagic one.

"Absolutely," he says.

He seems thrilled to have determined this. He has a sharp, well-shaped gray beard and a mustache of the same color. His right finger goes towards his mustache and I expect him to pet it thoughtfully, but instead he points directly at me.

"Rare for a stroke to be fatal. I wonder if there were other complications. Head injury perhaps?" he asks, almost accusingly.

I explain the fall, how gentle it was.

"Humph," he said. "Still, that concrete. So hard."

"He fell into my hands," I say. My face grows hot. Mrs. Sharma is looking at me with curiosity and I feel I have made a confession I should not have.

"I see," Dr. Venugopal says.

A waiter dressed in white comes around with spicy red dal. The Venugopals and Sharmas allow him to ladle some into the small stainless-steel bowls on their plates. I put my hand over mine to indicate that I do not want any.

"Such a genuinely nice couple they were," Mrs. Sharma says. "Imagine losing your husband like that."

She looks at me, a soloist among two couples, and says, "What I meant to say was, so suddenly."

Such comments don't upset me these days.

"It is lonely, but life goes on," I say, smiling.

Mrs. Sharma nods enthusiastically, relieved. The curls in her coiffed bob nod with her. Out of consideration, I change the subject.

"You look nice this evening," I say to Mrs. Venugopal. She is wearing a sleeveless block-print salwar kameez.

"Come shopping with me," she says. "I bought the material at Badshah. And I have a fabulous tailor."

I know she does not mean it. She sees how I dress. I wear ordinary clothes, and rarely buy new things. In any case, I would not spend my money at a place like Badshah.

"Better for the younger generation. Kamala might like to go," I say. "Though I suppose she isn't so young anymore."

The polite thing would be for Mrs. Venugopal to say that her daughter, Padmini, is also not so young, but she keeps silent and I feel like I have betrayed my child.

"Fantastic chicken korma today," Mrs. Sharma says, as she mixes it with her rice. She looks at the Fitbit on my wrist. "New gadget?"

"A present from my daughter," I say. "It counts your steps. Kamala says I must aim for eight thousand a day."

"We golf," Mrs. Sharma says. "We get plenty of exercise from that. No need to track it."

"Yes," I say.

In old age, status is tied to health, what you can do with your body and what you can't. Or sometimes, what you *say* you can do.

"Padmini bought Fitbits for us also. They want us to live long lives, don't they?" Mrs. Venugopal says.

"For what, I want to ask," Dr. Venugopal says, leaning forward. "For them?"

"Our son only visits every other year from California," Mrs. Sharma says.

"Padmini hardly comes," Dr. Venugopal says. His eyes catch mine and I see something childlike in them, something sorrowful. "I need another drink," he says.

"She is so busy," Mrs. Venugopal says. "This year she was promoted to director."

"But you know," Dr. Venugopal says, his voice a hush, "Renuka is moving." His eyes search my face. "Did you know?"

"No," I say, but immediately I understand. It happened

often to widows and widowers. She was moving abroad to join her children.

"Where to?" I ask. "Germany with her daughter, or Australia with her son?"

The worst would be if she had to split her time, I think to myself. A permanent temporary resident in two places.

"Neither," he says, his voice still quiet and conspiratorial. "She is moving back to Chennai. Her son and daughter are returning with their families, purchasing three side-by-side flats."

"But there are grandchildren?"

"Enrolling in our Indian schools."

Dr. Venugopal seems pleased that he has this information, that he is the one who is delivering it to me, Renuka's friend and witness to Mr. Swaminathan's death.

I have finished my food, and do not wish to stay through a second round of drinks.

"I am expecting a call from Kamala," I say, excusing myself.

Dr. Venugopal gives me a salute. "Best not to miss their calls. Otherwise, we may never catch them. Give her our regards."

I stand up and walk away. I hear Mrs. Venugopal say that Kamala lives in Alpharetta, and that Padmini lives in Buckhead.

"Thirty-minute drive," she says. "If there is no traffic."

•

When I get back to my flat, I call Kamala. It's Saturday morning there, one of the rare times I can be sure of reaching her.

"I had dinner with the Venugopals today."

"Lovely. I'm so glad you have friends there."

"I found out about a nice clothing store. We will go, you and me."

There is a pause, and then she says, "I may need to delay my trip."

"What for?"

"Work. What else?"

"We have a good Net connection. Come here and work."

"I'm sorry," she says.

"Forget about you," I say, unable to hide my frustration. "Do you ever plan to bring Veena here? Or will she always be too busy? She has not been to India since high school and now she is done with college."

"Of course she wants to come see you. Just not right now."

"Bring her to my funeral."

"Amma!" Kamala says.

I wish to hang up, but I think of my husband, and his palm on mine. I soften my tone.

"How is Veena?" I ask.

Kamala sighs.

"Still trying to sort out her life. She has a temporary job at the Georgia Aquarium."

"Doing science work?"

"No," Kamala says. "She cuts up the food for the animals."

Kamala goes on talking about her worries, how wayward Veena seems, but I stop listening.

I imagine my daughter's daughter as a butcher, chopping dead fish with bulging eyes for living fish with bulging eyes. I nearly comment that I know why Veena is so lost, how she needed her mother, how she still needs her mother. *Maybe if you had not worked so much*, I almost say. But once again, I remember my husband, the way he'd gently warn me to *stop*. I keep my mouth shut.

After Kamala, I could not have more children. My body tipped into menopause a decade earlier than expected, otherwise we would have given her siblings. But for Kamala, it was a choice. A second child would have been impractical, with her career to think of. The one to suffer was Veena, who spent all those hours in childcare, and then came home to that large, silent house, with all the toys and nobody to play with.

Now that I do not visit Alpharetta anymore—I find the journey far too draining—I must recall the house in my memory. The way the front hallway leads to the kitchen with the black-and-white granite counter, where, every day, I tried to make something tasty for Veena. How the family room is two carpeted steps down from the kitchen. How Kamala was always fearful I might trip on those steps. Halfway up the staircase to the upper level, there is a small landing, where Veena liked to launch marbles, to watch them roll and putter down the stairs.

When I close my eyes after hanging up the phone, I can hear the sound of Kamala's dishwasher, gushing and moaning late into the night, and her dryer, tossing clothes around and around.

For Mr. Swaminathan's kariyam, I wear a light orange Mysore silk sari. Subdued and traditional is best, based on what I know about Renuka. Still, I made sure to go for something colorful. It is a celebration, after all. The kariyam marks the fourteenth day after Mr. Swaminathan's death, the official end of the mourning period. Though the mourning never really stops. Not for a spouse. I finished knitting the sweater for Renuka, but I do not take it with me. What use will it be to her in Chennai, a city where the sun is glaring even on the coldest day of the year?

Mr. Swaminathan's kariyam is an efficient, in-and-out kind of affair, held not in the Swaminathan flat but in the Malliga Homes common lounge. Their flat is one of the more modest one-bedrooms, and would not have held the crowd. I arrive on time, but the priest has already finished the puja.

"Oh, we finished early," Renuka's daughter says breezily. "No need to make everyone sit through it. We wanted everyone to just enjoy food with us." She is a pretty woman in her thirties, with the same light green eyes as her mother. She is wearing an emerald choker around her neck and a peacock-blue silk sari that she keeps adjusting at the pallu. Children these days don't know how to wear Indian clothes well, I have noticed. Too much time spent in slacks and skirts.

"I heard you are moving back," I say.

"We are," she says.

I do not ask her questions. She has many people to visit with, and no idea who I am. I wash my hands and take a seat in the eating area, in front of an empty banana leaf, right next to Mrs. Sharma.

"Did you hear about the Bhatia scandal?" Mrs. Sharma asks me. "Didn't your husband work for them?"

"Yes. But I have not heard."

"Mrs. Bhatia is suing her own son, Brij, for two hundred crores. And her daughter, Cherry, for one hundred." She shakes her head. "Rich people. They have so much and they fight like this."

"I met her once," I say. "She seemed like a nice woman."

"Nice to everyone but her own," Mrs. Sharma says, her lips puckered in false sorrow.

Men holding stainless-steel buckets of food come by to serve us. I mix my sambar and rice together with my hands.

Simple food, but such a pleasure to eat something different than what the dining hall cooks prepare.

I speak with Renuka only once, on my way out. She is wearing a plain cotton sari. She has wiped off her bottu, taken off her earrings, bangles, and toe rings. She looks naked, and vulnerable. That is what happens. You wear these things for so many years, they become your permanent clothing.

"I am so sorry," I say.

"Thank you for coming," she says, a phrase she must have said many times already.

For the first time, I notice how many wrinkles she has on her face. All over, even across the bridge of her nose. Nevertheless, her eyes are as striking as ever, penetrating and thoughtful.

"He asked for you at the end," I say.

"I am glad you were there," she says softly.

A few days after Mr. Swaminathan's kariyam, I go Veg for dinner. They are serving dry, salted herring on the Non-Veg side. I simply cannot tolerate the smell these days, though I once loved it. I sit alone at a table for four in the back of the hall. I survey the room, all of us old people eating, and the listless waiters, wearing their starched white uniforms that grow less white by the day, moving from table to table.

The old should be with the young, the young with the

old. That was how it was for generations: babies sleeping in the armpits of their grandmothers, children sitting atop the shoulders of their grandfathers. Everyone in the same crowded home.

Nobody comes to sit with me today and I am glad for it. I might say something morose and develop a bad reputation. I finish my chapati and beans kottu, nicely sprinkled with freshly grated coconut, as quickly as possible, and rinse my hands at the tap.

My Fitbit says I need six thousand more steps before it gets dark. I do not walk my usual route. Instead, I walk to the side of Malliga Homes where the smaller flats are. Where Renuka's flat is. When I get there, I see that her gauzy yellow curtains are open. I look inside.

Empty.

She must have been so eager to leave. I turn the doorknob and find it unlocked.

I hear someone behind me, and turn around to find Renuka.

"I was just looking for you," I say. I quickly step out of her flat and shut the door, feeling guilty for the intrusion. "You must be leaving soon."

I watch her lift out a piece of green bean lodged between two teeth with her tongue. For a second, I wonder if her children changed their minds. They would remain abroad, and she with us, alone.

"Tonight," she says.

"I had made you a sweater for Australia, but I fear it will be of no use to you anymore."

"It was all so unexpected," she says. "I've always believed we must expect nothing from our children."

"My daughter is visiting next month," I say. "She plans to remodel our old flat in Chennai and live there. Perhaps you and I can walk along Elliot's Beach together one day."

"Oh!" Renuka says. She hugs me. "Children these days. They surprise me!"

I am shocked by her hug, and by my lie. I try to correct what I've said.

"You misunderstood," I say. "She is doing well in America. She just plans to visit often."

"I came to lock up," Renuka says pleasantly. "We need to sell this place so we can afford the new flats in Chennai."

"Do come by and pick up that sweater before you leave," I say. "Maybe you can use it after all, if you plan to go to the beach in the evenings."

"How I've missed it," she says. "That sea breeze."

I walk all around Malliga Homes until I reach eight thousand steps. I do not know why I lied to Renuka. Renuka, who lived in the smallest flat that Malliga Homes offers. Renuka, whose son is an ordinary movie theater manager. But she believed me. I imagine repeating the lie. To the Venugopals. To the Sharmas. To the chap who presses our clothes.

For some reason, I am reminded of my own father, who spent his final days in our flat in Chennai when Kamala was just a child. Toothless, he would sip his bland rice porridge and mutter an old Tamil proverb. "This is stranger than that, and that is stranger than this," he would say, as bits of the porridge dribbled down his chin.

It is dusk now at Malliga Homes. In that darkest part of twilight, that ungraspable moment before day turns fully to night, I pause to admire the oleander shrubs. Their white flowers, glowing at their yellow centers. The thick bougainvillea vines, in brilliant deep magenta, are creeping over the Malliga Homes compound wall. Some of the flowers are stuck on one side while others, by sheer luck, fall to the other.

A Life in America

For three decades, Chand gave his Indian graduate students his house keys when he and Raji left town. He told them to relax and use his spacious home as a place to rest and study, to use the hot tub in the back, and the grill, as long as they did not put beef on it. "Sleep in the guest bedroom," he said. "Escape your dreary apartments." It gave him pleasure to offer comforts that graduate student stipends could not afford. In his home, students could watch satellite channels like Zee TV and TV Asia, and catch up on episodes of *Koffee with Karan* and *Kaun Banega Crorepati*. Before Skype and WhatsApp and FaceTime, some students made long-distance phone calls from his landline. Chand never charged them for it. He treated them like family, because their own families were so far away.

He had been a graduate student in microbiology once, in Bozeman, Montana, tens of thousands of miles away from Vellore, his hometown in South India. Things were different then. When he moved to America, he called his parents once every three months, and was careful to think through what to say before dialing. Back then, calls cost three dollars for the first minute and one dollar for every minute thereafter. He remembered the loneliness, the immense sorrow that came from going months without uttering a word of Tamil. There was no way for him to express certain thoughts, certain feelings, in the English language. He remembered the warmth he felt when the one Indian professor on campus, a Punjabi chemical engineer named Dr. Mehta, occasionally invited him to his home for dinner.

In the early days, there had been almost no age difference between Chand and his students. He was like their older brother. When male students arrived, if they had no apartment to live in, he offered them the couch and a sleeping bag for as long as they needed it. He drove them to campus and took them out to lunch. With female students he was courteous and helpful, but careful not to be too friendly. He knew that lunch with an unmarried girl could easily be seen as something different than what he intended. When he turned twenty-nine, he flew to India and married Raji, his selection from a short list of potential brides his parents had made for him. He selected her for her sturdy build, and her steady gaze. Unlike the others, she did not look away when he spoke to her.

After Raji joined him in Pullman, they threw dinner parties for Indian graduate students several times a year. She cooked vats of food and sent students home with full stomachs and generous leftovers. Ziploc bags and Tupperware containers full of cinnamon and clove-infused pulao made with Basmati rice, and korma with coconut milk and ground cashew nuts. When a Hindu student and a Muslim student fell in love and failed to win the approval of their parents in India, he and Raji held a small wedding for them in their own backyard. The bride wore a strand of jasmine in her hair, made with flowers Raji ordered from Seattle.

Chand and Raji invited Indian graduate students over for all the holidays that Americans gather for, when foreigners don't know what to do. Easter, Christmas, Memorial Day, Labor Day, and Thanksgiving, which for years had been a festive, fusion meal in Chand and Raji's house. Their older son, Mo, always made turkey with black pepper brine. Raji and Deepa, Mo's wife, took care of the Indian food.

This year, no students expressed an interest in coming over for Thanksgiving. This did not surprise Chand. Grad students these days had more money. Flights were cheap, and Chand knew they liked to travel. Vegas. San Francisco. New York. What was unusual, though, was the call he got from an unknown number the Monday before the holiday. He was standing by the duck pond at Sunnyside Park with his family. His faded tan windbreaker, purchased at Marshalls twenty years ago, was zipped up to his neck to block the fall air. His four grandchildren were throwing stale pieces of bread into the pond for the ducks.

While he watched the birds fight over a particularly large piece of bread, his phone rang. The voice on the line explained that she was a reporter from the *Moscow-Pullman Daily News*.

"We have questions about your interactions with students," the reporter said.

"Sorry?" Chand said. "It's noisy here. Birds."

"Lawn mowing, dishwashing, running errands," she said. She sounded young, he thought, and spoke with an authority that only made her sound younger. "We've interviewed a number of your former Indian graduate students. They claim you made them do personal work for you against their will, that you never paid them. I'd like to hear your side of the story."

"You must have the wrong number." He felt his voice shift, squeak a little. He tried to make it lower and louder. "Bye."

A moment later, the reporter called again.

"Parties, shoveling, the flood," she said. "Remember the flood?" A flutter ran through his cheeks. How did she know these things? And why was she warping the truth?

"I don't understand," he said. "What is this?"

He walked to the other side of the park, stood near the metal door that led to the men's bathroom, and said, "Who have you been talking to?

"Listen," she said, "we will be running a story even if you don't talk to me. I'll text you my information. Please call if you would like to talk."

•

That evening in bed, he watched as Raji looked into a small round handheld mirror and plucked stray hairs from her eyebrows with the tweezers she kept on her bedside table, her nightly ritual. When she was done, he told her about the call. He kept his voice calm and his tone even. He spoke to her in Tamil, as he always did. She did not say anything aside from "And then?" each time Chand paused.

Her eyes were unreadable. He remembered how, years ago, she had asked him if it was improper for a student named Arun to be helping them with yard work every week.

"Once or twice is okay," she had said. "This is too much."

"We are like family," Chand had replied. "He has no problem with it. I told him it is only while my back is giving me trouble."

Now Chand said, "The best thing to do is stay silent."

When Raji looked at him but did not answer, he added, "Right? But I will tell John."

"Do you actually think he does not know?"

Chand sensed the irritation in her voice. John was the dean of Chand's college at the university, but he was also Chand's friend and longtime tennis partner. Raji had always thought John was the selfish type—that he acted chummy, but looked out only for himself.

"I doubt he knows," Chand said. He turned his bedside

light off. "He would have called. He's with family for the holiday."

Before he slept, Chand whispered. "Do not tell the boys yet. There is no need."

Two days after Thanksgiving, after Chand's sons and their families left, John called.

"I'm in Idaho. Bad phone service," he said. "Trust me, I wanted to call earlier."

John was in the Bitterroot Mountains, hunting for bears. He had taken Chand there once, to show him what it was all about. "I'll make a Westerner out of you yet," he said, and slapped Chand on the back. The mountains were thickly forested and steeply planed. The morning Chand went out with John and his cousins, the weather was beautiful. Then, midday, it started pouring without warning. The men in John's family traversed the land like they were mountain animals themselves, their sense of direction innate in spite of the poor conditions. Chand envied them.

He could picture John right now, wearing a green khaki shirt and gray pants, a Swiss army knife and headlamp in his side pocket.

"I tried to stop them back in October, Chandy," John said.

"You knew about it that long ago?" Chand asked. "Why

didn't you tell me? That reporter called and I was shocked. And you knew?"

"It got complicated, Chandy," John said. "We have to launch an investigation."

"Investigation?" Chand was in the living room, sitting on his leather armchair. He knew that Raji could hear him from the kitchen.

"We'll clear you," John said. "It'll all be over by January."

"Like two years ago?" Chand asked.

He heard another voice on John's end, in the background.

"Just a moment," John said to someone. "I'm almost done here."

"You'll get an official call soon," he said to Chand. "But I thought I should be the one to tell you."

John's words clung to Chand's skin. *Official call. Investigation.* "Who will take care of my lab? Just don't say Wenz."

John was silent.

"Don't say Banerjee," Chand said. "Don't."

"Probably Banerjee," John said. "I know what this must feel like. But he's the best we've got right now."

"You know he framed me! It had to be him," Chand said. "Just like last time."

"Hang in there," John said. "Take a deep breath. I'm here for you."

Not long after, a woman named Frances Chavez called

from the university's Ethics and Compliance Office to tell Chand he was suspended with pay until further notice.

"Your classes will be handled by another instructor. Your key card will be deactivated. A letter will be arriving in the mail," she said.

"Who?" Chand said.

"Excuse me?"

He raised his voice. "Who is my replacement?"

"I don't have that information. Even if I did, I'm afraid I would not be at liberty to share it with you."

"None of it is true," Chand said.

"Professor Chandra . . . er, Chandrasekharan, I understand this is difficult. You do still get your paycheck."

Mo and Murali called. Raji had told them. She could never keep anything from them.

"You need a lawyer," Mo said. He was upset. "You should have told me as soon as you knew."

"I was confused. I know nothing about these legal things."

"I'm a lawyer," Mo said. "Remember, you came to my graduation?"

Remember? I paid for it, Chand could not help thinking.

"You could have told me while I was carving the turkey," Mo said. "I'll send you some names."

"Can you be my lawyer?"

"I live in Virginia. You need someone there." His voice

softened, like he was reading a book to his preschooler and he repeated, "I'll send you names."

Murali, in contrast, was worried about Chand's health. He was a psychiatrist at Harborview Medical Center, in Seattle.

"Make sure you keep a schedule, Appa," he said. "This kind of stress can be life-threatening. Drink water. Go for walks."

"It's winter in Pullman."

"Wear a jacket."

"You are not my doctor."

"But I am *a* doctor," he said. "Just keep a routine. Any routine."

Afterwards, when Chand and Raji were having lunch at the dining table, he said, "The children act like I am someone they must put up with."

"They care about you," Raji said. "You misunderstand them."

Chand laughed. Raji looked at him and then down at his plate of rice and stew, as if the explanation for his laughter must be in the food. She shook her head at him, bewildered.

"What?" she said.

"Do you see?" he said. "This whole thing is a misunderstanding. Between me, and them, and everyone."

He fished a green moringa stick out of his stew with his finger. He sucked out the seeds and flesh. It was flavorless today, as bland as white rice, in spite of Raji's careful preparation.

After they finished their lunch, he helped Raji put the food away and load the dishwasher. He watched her. She had a quiet, elegant sort of beauty. She moved with confidence and kept her back straight as she worked. Her hair was short and curly, black with silver tones, and cut to the chin. At sixty-five, she was thoughtful about her looks, much more so than when she first moved from India to join him in America. She usually read for an hour or so after cleaning, but today, she and Chand sat on the sofa. He lay his head down on her lap, and she massaged his forehead with her thumb and index finger.

"What will we do?" he said.

"Call the lawyer. Then wait and see."

"I am being hunted," he said, before closing his eyes.

She took her fingers off his forehead. He felt her legs tighten under him.

"That is not what this is," she said.

The lawyer that Mo recommended was a woman he went to law school with, who had a practice in Spokane. Chand and Raji drove to her office early Tuesday morning. Valerie Shaw was a slender woman, tall with long red hair, pulled back into a clip. Her desk was large, made of cherrywood, and very high. There was no chair behind it.

"I stand when I work," she said. "But let's sit."

She pointed them towards a round table with four chairs,

by a window that overlooked the Spokane River. A pair of running shoes sat in a corner on the floor.

"It's important that you give me all the information you can," she said.

Chand handed her the papers that the university had mailed him, with details about his suspension and the investigation, and orders not to go to campus.

"Thank you," she said. "Now I'd like to hear your side."

Chand explained how he and Raji always treated students like family, how other faculty members were jealous—Wenz, Banerjee—how they had framed him.

Valerie smiled at Raji. "And how about you? What do you think of all this?"

"My husband is a good man," Raji said. "This should not be happening to him."

Valerie nodded. "Everything I'll be doing is based on that," she said. "That he's a good man, with good intentions. A man who followed the rules."

Chand handed a letter to Valerie. He was considering providing a written statement to the *Daily News* reporter.

"Absolutely not," Valerie said, skimming his text. "Do not talk to that reporter."

The article in the *Daily News* came out a week later. The day it was published, Chand woke up at 4 a.m. He sat on his leather armchair by the fireplace, sipping on a cup of hot water with lemon until he heard the newspaper thud against the door. He retrieved it from a half inch of fresh snow, pulled it out of its blue plastic sleeve, and rolled the rubber band off. Ink blackened the tips of his fingers. He looked at his picture on the center of the front page. It was a headshot the newspaper had taken five years ago, when he won the university teaching award. He took the paper with him into the kitchen, filled a glass with water, and took his diabetes medication. He turned on the light above the breakfast table and sat down to read.

"Professor Used Students as Servants for Decades," the headline read. Underneath, in smaller letters, "University Knew, Did Nothing."

For more than twenty-five years, the article said, "Dr. T. K. Chandrasekharan systematically took advantage of his position as a faculty member by bullying dozens of graduate students from his home country of India, coercing them to do work for his personal benefit." It went on, "Chandrasekharan, a renowned professor in the College of Pharmacy, has brought millions of dollars in grant funding to the university. This was perhaps why a related incident reported two years ago was covered up, according to sources familiar with the situation."

Chand collected saliva into a ball in his mouth and pushed it through the gap between his two front teeth. The "incident" two years ago had been nothing, over before it started. John had said so himself. A student had complained to the department about having to house-sit without compensation. So much had happened in the last two years that Chand had forgotten about it. Since then, he had won a major federal grant, published four papers, presented at half a dozen major conferences, and seen three former graduate students receive tenure at prestigious research universities.

According to the article, Chand had forced students to serve food and clean up after his parties, do yard work, shovel snow, and check his mail when he was out of town. It boldly pronounced, "In India, this sort of deferential behavior is the norm between students and teachers."

What could the *Daily News* possibly know about India? Chand puffed his cheeks and blew the air out slowly. "It was a sort of cultural exploitation on the professor's part."

His colleague Banerjee's name was not mentioned, but Chand knew he was responsible for the smear campaign. He had to be. Chand tried to be nice when Banerjee first arrived six years ago as an associate professor. Banerjee had been born and raised in Milwaukee, to Bengali parents; as a fellow Indian, Chand wanted him to do well. He invited Banerjee and his wife and children over for dinner. He went out of his way to chat with him in the halls and in the faculty lounge. But Banerjee took an early disliking to him. Chand could feel it. The avoidance of eye contact, the curt answers to questions, the false smile when they were face-to-face, whether it was at the office or at a party in the home of another Indian family. Chand then took his own disliking to Banerjee, this young man who lacked basic decency. And unlike Chand, Banerjee showed no special affinity towards Indian students. In fact, he seemed standoffish with them, never offering to see or help them outside of the college setting.

For all of his aloofness, Banerjee was popular in the Indian community. This perplexed Chand. Banerjee did not speak Hindi or Bengali and yet he and his pretty wife, a delicate-looking woman of Thai ancestry who wore saris with grace, were invited to all the parties other Indian faculty members threw. The Banerjees were equally at ease with the Indians from India, and the Indians who, like Mo and Murali, and Banerjee himself, had grown up in America.

Chand knew the precise point when Banerjee's dislike turned to hate. Two years ago, when Banerjee was up for tenure, Chand did not support it. His research was not strong enough yet, Chand told the committee. It was not a spiteful statement; it was true. Ultimately, Banerjee was given tenure anyhow. But Chand believed that Banerjee—in a fit of rage, after learning that his tenure had been threatened—convinced a student to file the house-sitting complaint.

Chand finished reading the *Daily News* article, showered, and dressed himself. It was still dark outside and Raji was sleeping. He left the newspaper on his desk in his basement study. No need for her to see it first thing. A small translucent spider ran across the paper. He caught it in his fist, and released it outside. Then—his pockets full of rolls of quarters he had withdrawn from the bank the day before—he drove around town and bought every copy of the paper that he could find in street corner stands. He could have paid a quarter and grabbed them all, but he paid for each copy that he took. *I have integrity*, he muttered to himself. He went to Bi-Lo when it opened at 7:30, and bought every copy there. So as not to seem odd to the cashier, he grabbed a box of orange Tic Tacs, and put it on the stack.

Next, he drove to IGA. In the parking lot, he turned the engine off. His mind wandered. He was at his house, some years ago, hosting a barbecue. "Hi, how are you? Welcome to Pullman. I'm Chand," he said, out loud. He turned the engine back on.

The supermarket could keep its papers. What was he doing? He was a professor. A man of science and logic. And now he was buying piles of newspapers, and talking to an imaginary student in his car. He drove away, angry and disturbed.

At home, he took the newspapers into the study and set them down on the floor of his supply closet, unsure of what else to do with them.

Raji came downstairs to check on him. She was already

dressed for the day, in pale green slacks and a black sweater. She looked calm. She surveyed the room, and spotted the stack of newspapers in the closet.

"Do you think people will not read the story if you buy every copy in town?" she asked. She pointed to her phone, which she held in one hand. "I read the whole thing this morning."

"Oh," he said. It was only Raji telling him, but he still felt his face grow warm with embarrassment.

"Never mind," she said. "Come upstairs for some tea."

"In a minute."

He shut the closet door. Even if he bought and burned every copy in town, people could still read the story on their laptops, on their phones, while waiting in line for a turkey sandwich at Stax, while sitting on the toilet.

The rest of the morning went by quickly. He and Raji fielded phone calls from friends who said they would stand by Chand. A few calls came from colleagues, though Chand did not answer those. Their elderly neighbor, Mrs. Lockney, called. Chand heard the old woman's voice croaking through the landline. "He's a good man," she said to Raji.

Geetha Hariharan called and asked Raji if she could help, since she and her husband were both professors. "I am not afraid to get involved," she said. Dr. Peruri, the oldest Indian professor in town, called Chand and said, "Jealous people are trying to make you look bad."

Arun called from Atlanta. Raji tried to pass the phone to Chand, but he shook his head. He did not want to talk to Arun yet.

Other former students called. "Would you speak in my favor? If needed?" Chand asked each one. They all said yes.

"We have many friends," Raji said.

But Chand saw it another way. Some people were *not* calling. Their friends who were also friends with Banerjee, for instance. And he had taught many students from India over the years. Only six called.

He pulled the article up on his phone. There were comments.

"We should have never let people like him come here," someone named "Local Washingtonian" wrote.

"Disgusting," was another comment, from "PROUD Coug Alum."

Chand wondered if he should post a comment anonymously, but thought that the lawyer, Valerie, would say that it was a terrible idea.

That evening, he and Raji sat in the living room, exhausted. Raji reading Agatha Christie on the couch, Chand flipping through channels on the television, half expecting to see himself on the nightly news.

He closed his eyes. He was at a summer barbecue again. Maybe the same one, maybe a different one. He had thrown so many. Arun was using tongs to flip the tandoori chicken, tinged red from cayenne and the dash of food coloring Raji put in the marinade. John was standing next to Arun, reaching for a nicely grilled leg with his fingers. Chand always invited John, and John often accepted. He loved Raji's chicken.

"Good, isn't it?" Chand said.

"What?" Raji asked, looking up from her book. "Did you say something?"

"Sorry. Nothing."

"Are you talking to yourself?"

The week after the article came out in the *Daily News*, *The Spokesman-Review* ran an article about Chand. Two days after that, it was *The Seattle Times*, and the day after, *The Chronicle of Higher Education*. Calls came from reporters at least once a day. Each time, Raji said Chand was not home. The *Spokesman-Review* reporter, a middle-aged man with a smile as friendly as a car salesman, showed up at their front door. Chand watched from the window upstairs as Raji shut the door in the man's face.

Valerie called and said she was preparing paperwork for him to sign, a formal complaint against the university for unfair treatment. "Don't talk to any reporters," she warned again.

Chand found it impossible to work on his grant proposal. Most mornings, he sat in his study after breakfast, rereading the *Daily News* article that started it all. Every day, he pulled a fresh copy of the newspaper out of the closet, highlighted the article's quotes in yellow, and then threw it in a plastic bin when he was done. Without classes to teach, without a lab to work in, this was his new routine.

He wore thermal socks to stay warm in the basement, and kept the door shut so Raji would know not to disturb him. Soon he had the article memorized, but still he reread it. He found that he craved it, same as his morning tea.

He shut his eyes and squeezed them tightly, wringing them for relief. Nothing came out.

He opened his eyes and kept reading.

"I felt threatened."

Chand dragged a highlighter over the words, a quote from a former student. The black ink smeared slightly from the pressure of his pen.

"He said our student visas would be revoked if we did not listen to him."

Had he really said that? If he had, it had absolutely been a joke. How could it have been mistaken for anything else? He tried to remember how and where, the exact words he might have used. Maybe it was at the Hariharans' annual Lakshmi puja. No, it was not at a puja. It was at another one of his summer barbecues. He could feel it. Hot grill. Warm sun. Blue skies. Smoky tandoori chicken. He had been feeling good-humored. He'd had a beer, maybe two. "Hey, if you want to keep your visa, you better eat this chicken and tell Raji it's good." Something like that. John was there, that time, too. John had laughed.

Chand kept reading. One student said he "felt like a slave," when Chand asked him to help clear the basement after the '92 floods. Chand remembered the flood, how the water collected on one side of their slightly slanted basement, soaking through two cardboard boxes of books in his study room closet.

Mo and Murali had been preschoolers then, and Raji was sick with pneumonia. It was a Sunday, and he could not find any help to hire. He put the boys into their blue station wagon and drove to the lab to make sure there was no flooding there. Some of his Indian students saw him carrying two children, one asleep, as he walked down the hallway. He never asked for help. They came on their own, and brought their friends. Everything was cleaned up in an hour. Chand took them to Pizza Hut afterwards, and ordered five Veggie Lovers deep dish pizzas and three pitchers of Pepsi to thank them.

Chand counted. There were seven former students quoted in the article. One current student spoke anonymously, complaining about having to load dishes after a party; he suspected this was Pramila, the modern girl from Mumbai who called Raji by her first name, instead of Raji Aunty. He looked at Arun's quote. Chand still owed him a call back.

"People may perceive things in a certain way, during

or after an incident," Arun had told the paper. "I never felt threatened. I always felt it was voluntary."

Chand used a green highlighter for Arun's quote, pressing so hard the marker squeaked. Somehow, he found Arun's quote more disturbing than the rest.

Arun had worked in Chand's lab for a year, then transferred to Georgia Tech, where he finished his PhD. It was a better fit for his research, and they had more funding for him. But during their short time together, Chand had grown fond of Arun. He came over often, and Mo and Murali liked playing basketball with him in the driveway. Arun was from Vellore like Chand; Chand's father and Arun's uncle had been Rotary Club friends.

Chand avoided leaving the house. The few times he did, he felt hollow, like a ghost. It did not help that it was early December, that time of the year when everyone acted lighthearted and happy, still optimistic about the season, not yet fully thrust into the holiday shopping frenzy.

"We need milk," Raji said, one day. She was sitting on the couch, and looked up from her reading. "Can you go to IGA?"

"No."

"You need to get out of the house," she said.

"I am playing tennis with John later today."

She took her glasses off and looked at him. "If you do not go, we cannot make tea tomorrow."

"Sorry." He shrugged.

Chand and John first started playing tennis together in 1988, the same year they both joined the university. Chand was the better tennis player and the better scientist, but time had shown that John always managed to pull ahead. They were the same height, around six feet, with similar builds, lean and stringy. As the years went by they even lost hair in the same pattern, leaving two white patches on the sides of each of their heads, causing John's wife to joke that they looked like brothers.

Chand shivered as he waited outside the field house for his friend. He had forgotten his gloves, and his hands felt stiff as he held on to his racket and bag.

"Sorry I'm late," John said breezily when he arrived. "Should we start? Have to dash to a meeting in an hour with the provost."

Chand was glad they were still playing tennis. It felt good to do one thing he had been doing before. It felt good to make contact with the ball, to hear its *pock* and watch it fly over the net and hit the court on the other side. Chand won the set easily. John's volleys, normally solid and surprising, were off, and kept landing beyond the baseline.

After the first set, they stood by the metal bench near the net where they left their bags. John drank a bottle of yellow Gatorade and Chand drank cold water.

"Hey," John said. His voice echoed through the field house. He lowered it. "Did you really ask ten students to empty your flooded basement with buckets? I hadn't heard about that one."

"They came because they wanted to. They offered. The paper has it wrong."

"We—I mean, they—are looking into everything," John said. He looked at Chand, his sharp jawline gleaming with sweat, his eyes thoughtful. "I've been wondering if you should resign before the hearing."

"Resign?" Chand asked. This had not even occurred to him. "I have a lawyer now. She is working on something," he said.

"I know. She's been in touch," John said. "I'm the dean, remember? I just don't think she can do much for you."

"What does that mean?"

"I was thinking out loud. Let's play."

"No," Chand said. "I want to know." He felt a twist in his stomach. A cramp.

"Look, you've brought in tons of money. I'm sure it will be fine. It was only a thought."

John tightened the cap to his Gatorade and set it down. He took a ball out of his pocket and bounced it on the ground. "Let's play."

John won the second set. The third was close, but Chand was out of energy, and John won again.

"I'm out of time today, Chandy," John said. He put his racket into its sleeve and picked up his bag.

Chand opened his wallet.

"You forgot the bill," he called out to John.

They had passed this two-dollar bill, now soft and well-creased, back and forth for years. The person who won the match held on to it until next time.

But John was already too far away. He tossed his empty Gatorade bottle into the trash and waved his hand at Chand. "Keep it," he said. "Can you get the balls?"

Chand squatted to the ground, picked up the balls one by one, and dropped them into the canisters. It was such a small thing, picking up tennis balls. He was always the one to do it after they played, though he'd never told Raji this detail. It would make her furious. But it had never bothered him, until today. *Think about resigning*, John had said.

On his way home, Chand felt guilty about the way he had spoken to Raji. He stopped by IGA and walked straight towards the back, where the milk was. He relaxed as he moved through the produce section, sensing that nobody was looking at him. They were all busy buying their groceries. Turning apples in their hands. Pulling single bananas off larger bunches. There was a pleasant melon scent in the air.

In the dairy aisle, his eyes scanned the rows of milk. Organic. Whole. 2%. They usually bought a half-gallon, since it was just the two of them. He decided to get a gallon so Raji wouldn't send him back soon. Though it wasn't too bad, being in the store. Feeling at ease in public for the first time in weeks, he took the longer route back to the register and grabbed some of the foil-wrapped mint chocolates Raji liked.

At home, he found her sitting on the couch with a cup of tea. She had a photo card in her hand.

"Holiday card from the Banerjees," she said. She handed it to him. There was a note written on it, in what looked like a woman's writing, soft and looping. "Raji and Chand—Wishing you all the best this holiday season. We hope to see you soon."

Chand tore it in half.

"You parked in the middle of the driveway," he said. "I couldn't get into the garage."

"I went out for milk, and when I was pulling in, my phone rang, so I parked quickly."

"I bought milk," Chand said. He held up the brown paper bag in his hand.

"After insisting you could not?"

"I was trying to be helpful."

"Hmmph."

"Who called?"

"Mo," Raji said. "I answer when my children call. He told me you did not pick up when he called yesterday."

"You think you are so good," Chand said. His anger surprised him. "You should have stopped me. You liked it."

"Liked what?"

"Having students come over. Having them do things. If I am guilty, then you are, too."

"Stop," she said. He saw that she was on the verge of tears. He could always tell when it was happening: the swallow in her throat, half-formed, and the pooling in her eyes, ready to spill over. But he could not stop.

"Leave, if you think I am so terrible," he said. "Stay with Mo or Murali. Visit your sisters in Chennai."

"Who do you think I am?"

She was going to stand up and walk away, he knew it. There was nothing he could do. She *should* walk away, he thought. He had ruined this, too.

But she stayed put, and somehow caught hold of herself, though the pools in her eyes remained.

"It is too late to talk about whether I tried to stop you or not," she said in a clear voice, each word sharp and succinct. "All that has happened has already happened."

On Christmas Eve, Chand pulled down the typed list of phone numbers and addresses that he and Raji kept on the fridge door, nervously pocketing the magnet that held it up.

He found Arun's number and dialed it.

"Chand Uncle," Arun said. "How are you? I'm so sorry about all this."

It had been a comfort, to know he had at least Arun.

"Arun, am I a bad person?"

"You must not think such things," Arun said.

"But did I force you to do yard work?"

"I was volunteering my time."

A half-truth was still a lie, Chand thought. It was the worst kind.

"If you had told me I was doing something wrong, I would have been more careful," Chand said. "I treated you the way I treat my own kids. That's how I treated all of you."

"Of course, Uncle, I should have said something," Arun said.

"Your transfer from the university. Did you leave because of me?"

He was grasping. This was what he had been scared to ask Arun for weeks. If he did not ask, he had a way out. He could believe for the rest of his days that the paper was wrong, that Banerjee was wrong, that every student who spoke out against him was wrong.

"No, no. I left for my research," Arun said.

It was a half-truth.

"Not because of me?" Chand asked.

There was a pause. "Of course not, Uncle."

After they hung up, Chand turned around to see Raji in the door frame. She had been listening.

"It's over now," he said. She put her arms around him. She was more than half a foot shorter than him, so as she squeezed him close he turned his head sideways to press his cheek to the top of her head, inhaling the scent of the amla oil in her hair. She was there, with him.

What could he count on as the facts in his life? A career, a woman, two children. A house. A life in America. Hundreds of students. For all of this, there was plenty of evidence. But what about the truth of who he was, of how he had lived? There was no accounting for this, exactly, on paper. This was not a question of salary, of summation, of awards or grants. It was a feeling, a sense of himself that he once had, that was being erased and rewritten without his consultation.

He felt the warmth of Raji's body against his.

"I am here," she said.

Chand emptied his office after New Year's. There was no party, no cake, no farewell. It went into the books as a resignation, so his pension remained intact; the lawyer negotiated that for him. He had worked long enough to earn this. The house was paid off, and he and Raji qualified for Medicare. Financially, he had nothing to worry about.

In the days and months that followed, he went for long walks. He played tennis with John occasionally. He could not read anything scholarly—that level of concentration was gone, and he did not know if it would ever return. He and Raji were still invited to some parties, though he suspected they were excluded from others. If she suspected the same, she never mentioned it. When Mo and Murali called, Chand held the phone for as long as they spoke, showing no hurry, but it was impossible to really listen.

One morning in mid-April, Chand woke and went downstairs to the breakfast table. He sat across from Raji, who had just finished her cup of tea. They were quieter these days, orbiting each other without ever colliding. She started talking to him—telling him about the new mystery she was reading, about the new chairs at the senior center, about pictures of the grandchildren that Mo's wife had sent.

"Are you listening?" she asked. "Should I say it again?"

He tried to remember what she was talking about. Some of her eyelashes were going gray. Some of her eyebrow hairs too. He had never noticed this before. How quickly she was aging, and yet how beautiful she remained. He took a breath.

"No, keep going, Raji," he said. "Tell me about the book."

Buddymoon

The wedding is in Pullman, a town that Gauri, fifty-nine years old now, has not visited in more than a decade. She flies from San Francisco to Seattle, and drives down I-90 in her economy-size rental car. It was too costly to fly directly into the town's two-gate airport, or even Spokane's slightly larger one. The five-hour journey from Seattle is as she remembers it: tolerable for the first two and a half hours, and then, after Ellensburg, flat, straight, and endless. She fiddles with the car stereo and finds that it is broken. As a family, when they had been a family, she and Kamal and the kids had driven this route dozens of times in their aqua Toyota Camry, to get to Seattle Airport, to buy Indian groceries, to visit the Hindu temple. Once, she and Kamal took the girls to Seattle for spring break, and they went to Mount Rainier and the science center. Anita was five years old and, on the drive back, pointed a finger to an empty stretch along the highway and said, "If somebody died here, nobody would know." This morbid observation from the mouth of a toddler threw

Gauri, Kamal, and consequently Sahana, age three, into a long fit of giggles, ending with Sahana wetting her pants. The oval stain she left never scrubbed out of the backseat.

Today, when Gauri passes Ellensburg, her cheeks tingle. Underneath her jacket and her long-sleeve shirt, her arms turn cold. She is almost home. A once-upon-a-time home, at least.

The feeling that she has is not déjà vu, though this is the phrase that comes to mind because it is the name of the strip club she passes after Ellensburg. Déjà Vu is the only structure in sight aside from windmills, barns, and silos. Today the board says, "Girls and Steak Special." As she gets closer to her destination, rolling wheat fields appear on either side of the road. And then, at last, a familiar crimson sign with wooden letters bursts into view: "Welcome to Pullman, Washington. Home of the Cougars."

When the girls were younger, Gauri flew into Spokane from San Francisco twice a year to see them. She would pick them up in Pullman and drive right back to Spokane, where they did "city weekends," as the girls called them. She told Kamal it was because there was more to do in Spokane, but really it was to avoid the gaze of old friends and neighbors in Pullman. Gauri was short and slender; back then, strangers mistook her for a babysitter or an older sister. Childbirth had not widened her hips or given weight to her breasts. Sometimes, she and the girls went to Silverwood to ride roller coasters and eat cotton candy, or to the AMC to watch movies, each of them holding their own tub of salty popcorn, dripping with extra butter. They went to the Olive Garden, where they filled up on breadsticks and salad before the cheesy eggplant Parmesan and linguine arrived. They took the entrees back to the hotel, stored them in the mini-fridge, and reheated them in the lobby microwave the next day. Gauri took Anita and Sahana to the mall, since Pullman did not have one, and let them buy whatever they wanted. If she maxed out one credit card, she pulled out another. Sahana approached shopping with a painful focus, as if it were official business. Anita was jollier, more casual about it. But both girls always emerged from the stores equally tired and happy, their hands firmly gripping large shopping bags. At night, the three of them fell asleep on the same bed after drinking hot chocolate from the machine in the lobby.

Their life with their father was mundane, ordinary, necessary. Gauri wanted life with her to be a vacation. She was the holiday parent, after all.

Once, when she came to Pullman to pick the girls up, they were not ready. They were nine and eleven, and only a few years had passed since the divorce. Sahana was looking for her stuffed pig, and Anita was searching for a Nancy Drew book.

"I need to finish it today, Mom," Anita said, the desperation clear in her voice.

"Have a cup of tea," Kamal said. "Give them a few minutes."

She left her shoes at the door and went in. The tea was

good, milky and nicely steeped with ginger and cardamom. But it had been awkward to sit with her ex-husband like that, at the same dining table where she had served hundreds of meals when she was his wife. She was surprised by how organized the house was, as if it hadn't needed her in the first place. Kamal was not a decorator, but he was tidy and neat. The cabinets and drawers were labeled with white stickers printed on a label maker. The sink was empty, the dishwasher running. Beans simmered in a slow cooker on the counter.

Kamal had kept his distance after the divorce, never inquiring about Gauri's finances or the Harish situation, always keeping their interactions strictly about the girls. She paid a small amount in child support every month—less than one hundred dollars. She was mostly regular about it, though when she was late, he said nothing. He had managed to make a clean break, without alienating their daughters from her. But this meant that there was nothing to fight about or discuss in detail. Everything related to the girls was addressed over e-mail or a short phone call, brief interactions that left Gauri feeling hollow, like her personal life was a business matter. After that uncomfortable tea, Kamal never invited her in again. The girls were always waiting by the door for her when she arrived, pigtailed and dressed alike, with their small, identical suitcases. Sahana was short and chubby, with Gauri's droopy eyes and pencil-thin lips. Anita was taller and lean, with thick, dark eyebrows like Kamal. He always had snacks packed for them too. Tiny oranges, Ritz crackers, carrot sticks.

At the front desk of the Holiday Inn Express, Gauri places a paper cup under the glass water jar and turns the stainless-steel spigot. She spells her name out to the brown-haired young man behind the front desk for the third time. "S-E-L-V-A-M," she says, "M not N."

"I'm not seeing it," he says, frowning.

Selvam is Kamal's last name, but Gauri did not change it after the divorce. At first, she kept the name because she did not want to rehash her failed marriage with every credit card company, airline, and the DMV. Later, it felt like too much effort to make the change.

The receptionist looks at Gauri, his frown replaced with a cheerful, can-do smile.

"Are you a guest of the bride or the groom?" he asks.

"I have a room here," Gauri says. Her voice rises a little when she says "room." She knows she sounds weak and unsure of herself. Kamal had told her the room was taken care of.

"It's the least I can do," he had said. "You're coming all the way here."

"Hmmm," the receptionist says. "Wait. I have a Gauri Nataraj."

"That's me," Gauri says. "Maiden name."

She puts her driver's license back in her wallet. "But I don't have an ID with that on it."

"No problem!" he says, still smiling. "I trust you." He hands her a key. "You're on the top floor. The treats in the room are compliments of the bride's father."

Gauri rolls her luggage into the elevator and presses the button for the fifth floor. The room is basic but clean, with a queen bed and simple furniture made of darkly stained wood. On the desk, there is a bag of spicy cashews and a miniature bar of artisan chocolate from the local factory. Fancy but small, she thinks.

A note is attached to the cashews with red ribbon. "Thank you for coming to the wedding of Anita Selvam and Samuel Randall," it says. "We look forward to celebrating with you."

Gauri has not met Samuel, but she has studied his pictures carefully. He has chestnut-colored hair, and though his hairline is receding, his face is youthful and clean-shaven. He looks like a kind, happy man. Gauri suspects that he has a tendency to put on weight, which could be problematic, but he also seemed like he knew how to enjoy a good meal, and the thought of this pleases her. He has a small scar that runs down the side of his cheek. A childhood ski accident, Anita had told Gauri on the phone. "It's more visible in pictures than in real life." Gauri runs through a mental list of the few other things Anita has told her about him: he is twenty-nine, a former college soccer player, and he owns and runs the shoe store his grandfather started, in Hartford, Connecticut, where Anita is a medical resident. Anita is a runner, and one day she wandered into the store to buy new shoes. Samuel slipped a pair onto her feet and said, “They fit just right.” This detail Gauri knows from Samuel and Anita’s wedding website.

From Anita, Gauri also knows that Samuel’s father is dead, and that his mother has Parkinson’s. She is wheelchair-bound and her speech is slurred. She lives in a nursing home near the shoe store.

“But she understands everything,” Anita told Gauri on the phone. “She is so happy for us.”

“So am I,” Gauri replied.

The wedding website tells the story of the proposal. It happened in the shoe store, one evening after closing. Samuel hid his grandmother’s ring in a pair of black dancing shoes that he presented to Anita. Afterwards, their favorite Beatles song, “Something,” played on the store’s speakers and they danced, moving around the shoe displays as if they were in a crowded ballroom.

“I would love to meet him,” Gauri told Anita on the phone.

“The wedding is in six months, Mom,” Anita said. “You’ll love him.”

“Did Dad meet him?”

“Yes,” Anita said. “Samuel came to Pullman last year.”

Gauri took a deep breath.

"Maybe I can come to Hartford one weekend."

"I'll check my schedule," Anita had said. "You know my hours. And weekends are busy at the shoe store."

Gauri hangs up her sari for the wedding and her dress for the reception in the hotel room closet. She opens her red purse and checks the contents of the small velvet-covered jewelry box she has been carrying around. She kicks her tennis shoes off and lies on the bed. She closes her eyes and rests, as most of an hour goes by. The ceremony is the next morning. If there is an event on the eve of the wedding, she was not told about it. She looks at her phone, considers calling Sahana or Anita, or even Kamal. Maybe they were doing something fun, laughing together. She wants to be with them. But if they wanted to see her, wouldn't they have called?

Briefly, she considers calling someone else in Pullman, her old friend Geetha, maybe. Instead, she orders a small pizza with bell peppers, onions, and jalapeños, and eats it in bed with just the bedside light on. Then she pulls the heavy comforter over her and falls asleep.

When Gauri lived in Pullman, there were only ten other Indian families in town. She and Kamal were closest to two other couples: Geetha and Bhaskar Hariharan, and Seema and Raj Jain. The families met often, gathering for potlucks in one another's homes. The men discussed current events—the Gulf War, Oklahoma City, O.J.—while they hungrily dug into their food with their hands, breaking off pieces of puri and dipping them into vegetable korma or chana masala, masterfully allowing their fingertips alone to get sullied. The children, all under ten, sat on old bed sheets, spread out on the floor while they ate. When the kids were finished, the women took their place. After dinner, the adults drank Kashmiri tea and everyone ate desserts. Sometimes it was jiggly mango pie set in a Keebler graham cracker crust, sometimes it was spongy rasgullas floating in rose-flavored sugar syrup, often it was just vanilla ice cream.

Those dinners with friends went on for hours, until the youngest children fell asleep in front of the television or in their mothers' laps. When Gauri and Kamal hosted in their home, the reverberations of their friends' laughter remained long after the parties ended, bouncing gently off their walls, elevating their mood and fueling the erotic in them. After they put the food away, washed the dishes, and double-checked that the kids were fast asleep, Kamal would massage her shoulders and then, in the bedroom, slowly strip her of her clothes as he kissed her, his mouth still spicy from the evening's meal.

Gauri and Kamal were the first fracture. A few years later, the Jains moved away. The Hariharans stayed on in Pullman, and made other friends as more Indian families moved to town. The dinners did not last.

•

Gauri enters the botanical garden alone, wearing a rose-colored silk sari with a green border, a gift from Kamal's parents at the time of their wedding. She follows a trail of stepping stones set in grass, clutching her red purse, her eyes darting. A photographer snaps her picture. Wincing, Gauri adjusts her sari's pleats. She remembers the family photos they took here, at Lawson Gardens. They were good ones.

Now there are chairs set up in rows, with an open aisle down the middle, leading up to a gazebo full with dangling purple wisteria. There is no pandal at the gazebo, no holy fire to walk around. No place for a Hindu priest to sit. There is only a microphone, attached to a tall stand. There is a meadow of tulips behind the gazebo, and to the left of this, a circular rose garden with alternating hues of pink, red, and white. Gauri purses her lips. This is Pullman's only public garden. It has to do everything at once.

The guests are not here yet; Gauri is early. She sees Kamal standing with Samuel in the rose garden. Kamal waves to her and walks her way. He is wearing a crisp green kurta with billowy white cotton pants. His hair is gray and he has slight breasts now. Otherwise, he looks to Gauri as he always has since their divorce: handsome enough and serious, but content.

"Come meet our groom," Kamal says.

Samuel embraces Gauri. He is wearing a well-tailored black suit and a red tie.

"Gauri," he says. "I've wanted to meet you for so long."

"Me, too," she replies, wishing she could think of something more meaningful. This was her chance to make a good first impression. Instead she cannot help but stare at the scar. Despite Anita's claim, it is just as visible as it is in pictures.

"Ski accident," Samuel says, and Gauri's cheeks flush with embarrassment.

"You look lovely," Kamal says to her. Their eyes meet and she knows that he means what he says. He had always found her attractive. He puts his hand on her back and she feels the light pressure of his palm through her sari blouse. She swallows at the contact. It is so painful. A second later, his hand is gone, and she wants it back.

"Anita is getting ready," Kamal says. "I'll take you there." His eyes drop to the red purse in her hand. "You still have that old thing? Didn't I give that to you?"

On the way to the dressing room, he points to a row of chairs in the front. "Those seats are for family," he says.

"Me?" Gauri asks.

"Obviously. You are the mother of the bride."

Gauri knocks on the dressing room door. Sahana opens it and embraces Gauri lightly and briefly, without any ceremony. "Mom!" Anita says. "You're here."

She rises from an upholstered chair and hugs Gauri tightly. Gauri is surprised to find that Anita is wearing neither a traditional red sari nor a white wedding gown. She is wearing a strapless red dress made of layered taffeta, the same shade as Samuel's tie. Sahana is wearing a royal-blue satin dress, its straps as thin as shoelaces.

"I brought you something," Gauri says. Her fingers fumble with the zipper on her purse for a second, but she opens it and takes out the velvet-covered jewelry box. She hands it to Anita. "These belonged to my mother."

Anita opens it while Sahana stands next to her. Inside, there are diamond earrings, in the shape of six-petaled flowers.

"I remember these," Anita says. "Thank you."

"I did not tell you beforehand," Gauri says hesitantly. "You don't have to wear them today."

"I'll wear them," Anita declares, smiling at Gauri. "Dad bought me a new necklace. These will match."

"You already have earrings that go with the necklace," Sahana protests. She shakes her head. "Don't make a last-minute change."

"It's okay," Anita says. She looks at Sahana and then takes a step closer to Gauri. "This way I can wear something from Mom and something from Dad."

Kamal asked for a divorce on a Monday afternoon in April. Anita was at school and Sahana was napping after a half-day of kindergarten. Kamal had called to tell her he was coming home for lunch, something he did often to avoid the cafeteria food. Gauri prepared rice and chicken korma and plantains sautéed with onions. He said it after she served him a plate full of food, after she sat down in front of her own plate. She had just molded together a ball of korma and rice with her fingertips and was about to put it into her mouth.

Later she would have many questions, but in the moment, she only managed a few through her tears.

How long had he felt this way?

What had she done wrong?

Could they fix the problem?

"I don't love you," he said, so matter-of-factly that he may as well have been talking about their water bill. "Not in the way I should."

He had figured this out within months of their wedding, and had known it for sure by the end of the first year, he said.

"A marriage of convenience is not for me, even if it works for our friends," he said.

"You never seemed unhappy."

"Our parents will be upset," he said. "But I will take the blame."

"The girls," she said.

"I love the girls."

"Then why are you saying this? How could you do this?"

"I am not a necessity in your life."

"How can you speak for me?" Gauri said.

A nauseous feeling swept through her, from her throat to

her stomach, that same ill sensation that came on during the first trimesters of her pregnancies.

Gauri and Kamal's marriage had been arranged by their parents, a match based on horoscopes. He was already in America for graduate school and flew to India just days before the wedding. Until the wedding, she knew him only as a mustached man in a photograph, wearing brown slacks and a slate-colored polo shirt, standing with a backpack slung over his shoulder in front of a brick building that said "College of Sciences."

"It's for the best," Kamal said. "Time will make it okay."

Gauri pushed her plate away, the food mostly uneaten. By then, the tears had spread across her face. Thick strands of hair stuck to her cheeks and forehead.

"Did we marry for love?" she asked. "Is that what you thought?"

Even as she said this, she found herself wondering what he meant by love, exactly, if it was not what they had shared. What about all those times he had touched her? Leaned into her hair and kissed her head? Whispered into her ear, cupped her breasts, fit his body over hers? She loved him, she loved being with him, and she had no reason to think that he felt differently.

Their friends were as stunned as Gauri when they heard the news. They tried to counsel Kamal out of it, first questioning his reasons, then shaming him for abandoning his young wife. Geetha hosted an amateur therapy session in her split-level home. While Anita, Sahana, and the other kids played in the basement, the men talked in the living room and the women went upstairs to the master bedroom. Gauri sat on the center of the bed, legs crossed, with the other two women on either side of her.

"Is he having an affair?" Geetha asked.

"No affair," Gauri said. She glared at Geetha, aware that she was feeling defensive of Kamal, of her marriage, in spite of what was happening. "He just does not like me."

This was inconceivable to her friends, for there had been no sign of this dislike at any get-together, at any party.

"What do you mean?" Seema asked. "You have two children. You have friends. You have a home."

"Oof. He sounds like an American," Geetha said. "On a quest for 'true love.'"

As Gauri left Geetha's house with Kamal and the girls, she heard Seema say to her husband, "Everything seemed so normal."

This is a line that Gauri has never forgotten. She thinks of it when she sees young couples, dressed up and walking into restaurants together, sharing a glass of wine, playing with each other's fingers at the table. They, too, seemed so normal. How many of them would one day split up, declare that it was never meant to be? Claim that something was wrong from the beginning? She thinks of it, too, when she sees elderly couples, whose sense of commitment has surely outlasted their love. And she cannot help but think of it, of all of it, moments before Anita weds Samuel.

Gauri sits next to Sahana and Kamal during the ceremony. Half the guests are in saris and kurtas, the other half in dresses and black suits. The ceremony is unlike anything Gauri has seen before. Instead of a priest or a minister, there are two officiants, no older than Samuel and Anita. Gauri does not recognize these friends, one male, one female, both dressed in black suits, but the program says their names are Karla Lin and Eric Hunt. After Karla and Eric read from the papers in their hands, Samuel and Anita exchange vows.

"I will always be at your side," Samuel says.

"We will create a home filled with love and compassion," Anita says.

Gauri looks down at her red purse and tries to smoothe out the wrinkles that have formed in her sari. She nearly laughs out loud when she hears the vows, because she is sitting next to Kamal, and no such promises had come true for them. It occurs to her that this strange, agnostic ceremony is happening not because her daughters have rejected Hinduism or Indian culture, but because—between Kamal's house in Pullman, and her studio apartment in Fremont, and no trips to India—the girls have no real culture at all.

No traditions of their own, none instilled by Gauri or Kamal, anyway.

After the ceremony, there are pictures. Anita wants Gauri to be a part of them. "Stand next to Samuel," Anita says.

"Closer, please," the photographer says. "You're all family, now." Gauri shifts until her arm touches Samuel's coat sleeve.

A woman of Kamal's height, and about the same age as Gauri, is standing to the side, watching. She has short blond hair, toned arms, small breasts. She is wearing a long sleeveless yellow dress. Gauri feels the woman's gaze on her. Though neither Sahana nor Anita, nor Kamal, has said a word about her, Gauri instantly knows who she is.

After the pictures are taken, Kamal walks up to the woman and motions for Gauri to come towards them.

"This is Christine," he says. "Christine, this is Gauri, Anita and Sahana's mother."

Kamal puts his arm around Christine's waist. They look comfortable together. Christine has never given birth to a child, Gauri can tell not because of her figure, but because of the ease in her eyes. Not a worry in the world. Christine is wearing heels. She is not as tall as Kamal after all.

"Christine teaches accounting at the university," Kamal says.

"Nice to meet you," Gauri says. She extends her hand. Christine ignores it and steps forward to hug her.

"I've heard so much about you," she says. When she

smiles, her blue eyes brighten. She seems frustratingly genuine. "Your children are beautiful," she says.

After Kamal asked for the divorce, he said he would find an apartment for himself nearby. Gauri said no.

"If you get to end this, I get to decide how," she said. In spite of the terror, and the pain, she felt thrilled by the idea of finding a place to call her own. All her life, she had lived with either her parents or with Kamal. She moved out of their three-bedroom house on Military Hill and into a one-bedroom apartment walking distance to campus. To keep life as stable as possible for Anita and Sahana, she gave Kamal custody. The house would be the girls' primary residence.

Gauri enrolled in programming classes at the university, though she had no background in computer science. It was Kamal who had given her the idea, when she was packing up.

"Programming is the next big thing," he said.

"I don't know anything about computers."

He shrugged, picked up a box, and took it to the front door. "I'm not trying to tell you what to do."

The following week, Gauri signed up for two courses. One called Introduction to Programming, and another called Java for Novices.

She met Harish in her Java class. He was the instructor. He had moved from India to pursue his master's degree two years prior. While he searched for a full-time job, to make ends meet, he also worked at the Mediterranean Grill, where he spent hours pulling hot pita bread out of the oven. One of the first things Gauri noticed about him was that he smelled of gyro and falafel. She would learn that he smelled this way even after he showered, even on the days he didn't work. It was alluring, a man who smelled like food. Kamal had never cooked for her.

After class one day, Harish approached her.

"How do you like it so far?"

The following week, he asked, "Want to get some coffee?"

Their romance was swift and surprising. He was a Punjabi from Delhi, a city boy. Her father was a cotton farmer in Tamil Nadu. She did not know Hindi. He did not know Tamil. She was thirty-four. He was twenty-five. If she had looked her age—if he knew she was mother to two children—perhaps he would have stayed away. But he mistook her for an undergraduate, and by the time he took her out and learned her story, they were both too smitten to walk away.

She took him to her apartment that day after coffee and used cream of wheat to make him upma sprinkled with roasted cashews. They ate the savory porridge with mint chutney she already had in the fridge. Afterwards, they sat on the blue futon sofa in her living room and he ran his fingers up and down her arms, causing her to shiver with pleasure.

She was embarrassed and taken by how playful he was,

confident in his touch. He marveled at her willowy body, exclaimed that he could tell she was flexible. To prove his point, he grabbed her foot, tried to thread it through her crossed arms.

"See? You're a pretzel," he said, and before she could laugh he surprised her by kissing her, parting her lips with his tongue.

Two months later, he found a job in California.

"Come with me," he said.

Gauri gave notice to her apartment manager, and called Kamal to tell him of her plans.

"You are running away with a man you just met, leaving two little girls here?"

"Were you pretending, all of those times we were together?" Being with another man had emboldened her to ask, her modesty no longer a barrier. "Every time?"

"That was lust, Gauri," Kamal said. "A different thing."

She twisted the phone cord around her hand and then let go.

"I will visit the girls," she said. "I will still be their mother."

The girls sobbed when Gauri said goodbye. Before she climbed into Harish's rusty two-door Honda, Sahana jumped onto her, wrapped her legs around her waist, and clung to her neck. She was seven years old, but Gauri held her like a toddler.

"I will hate you if you leave," she said, her face twisted with grief. "I will hate you forever."

Eventually Gauri pried Sahana off her body, and handed her to Kamal. Sahana cried into his shoulder while he looked at Gauri with pursed lips. Anita, age nine, sat on the front porch step with her face buried in her arms. She refused to talk. "I'll be back, babies," Gauri said.

Sahana looked up. "If you come back soon, we won't stay mad."

After the wedding, Gauri returns to the hotel to rest and change for the evening. The reception is in the ballroom of the university's student union building. It is the largest venue in town, the only place that can hold all two hundred guests, triple the number invited to the morning ceremony. Gauri enters at the ground level. She walks past the bowling alley and the eatery selling burgers and fries. She takes the elevator upstairs. She is wearing a sparkly green dress with short cap sleeves and a V-neck. The dress had seemed like a good idea when she bought it, when the saleswoman at Nordstrom's convinced her to spend the two hundred dollars. "You're a young, beautiful mother of the bride," the woman said. But the dress feels scratchy and tight now. Gauri fidgets with the shoulders and tugs at the sides.

A voice calls out to her. "Gauri!"

It is Geetha. She is wearing a blue silk sari, her hair pulled back into a taut bun. Gauri feels a rush of gratitude that she has not become fat and old-looking, like her friend. Geetha's skin is darker than Gauri's, and she wears a coat of foundation on her face that is a few shades too light. When they were younger, Gauri envied how efficient Geetha was at balancing career and family, securing tenure while nursing babies and keeping a clean home. But the years have taken a physical toll on her friend in a way that they have not on her.

When Geetha hugs her, her soft stomach folds press into Gauri's lean body.

"It's been ten years, and you haven't changed a bit," she says to Gauri.

Instinctively, Gauri touches her forehead. She knows there are lines where once there were none.

"Neither have you," she says.

Geetha laughs. "I left you a message last month. I told you to stay with us."

"Kamal booked me a room," Gauri says.

"I know. I asked him."

"Sorry I didn't call back."

"He has done a fantastic job. With all of this, but also

with the girls." She looks at Gauri. "You have, too." Then she adds, "I never see him these days, you know."

"No dinner parties?" Gauri asks.

"Oh, I have parties. I invite him," Geetha says. "He stopped coming long ago."

"Maybe he feels strange, coming alone."

Geetha smiles just slightly. "Who says he has to come alone?"

After Anita started high school, the girls flew to California to visit Gauri once a year, in the summer. She was a customer service consultant for a large department store. Her job was to answer phone calls, take orders, and troubleshoot when needed. A boring job, but she was good at it, and the pay made things just barely manageable for her. She lived in a small studio in Fremont, with a two-burner stove. Harish was long out of the picture by then, having left her to marry a younger woman.

The girls loved taking BART from Fremont to San Francisco, where they walked up and down hills, and ducked in and out of novelty stores. They loved, too, that there were Indian restaurants in Fremont. Gauri took them out for butter chicken and malai kofta and fresh naan made in the tandoor, North Indian dishes that the girls rarely had a chance to eat. There were no Indian restaurants in Pullman or Spokane, and Anita and Sahana had not visited India since the divorce. There never seemed to be time, and both Kamal and Gauri worried that the girls would be seen as pathetic by the extended family: children whose parents could not hold it together, not even for them.

One summer, just before Sahana's freshman year of high school and Anita's junior year, the Fremont studio suddenly lost its charm. Behaving less like a vacationer and more like an uptight guest, Anita kept cleaning, scrubbing and wiping Gauri's kitchen with rags and dish soap, her sleeves rolled up, her hair pulled back into a high ponytail. She ran the Dustbuster daily, though no amount of vacuuming could give life to the dull orange carpet.

"I've never seen a layer of sticky dust on plants before," Anita muttered to Sahana one day, as she wiped the leaves with damp paper towels. Gauri winced. She had tidied up a bit before the girls came, but living alone had made her careless. She could not see her own filth.

"Does your father keep the house clean?" Gauri asked.

"Not really," Anita said quickly.

"Why are you lying?" Sahana said. "We clean it together every Sunday."

Gauri was stung, both because Anita felt like she needed to lie, and because Sahana felt like she didn't.

It was Sahana who hurt Gauri the most. Like Kamal, Sahana seemed to have given up on her. She was sullen and distracted, always typing on her laptop, sending instant messages to friends. If Gauri said, "Thai or Chinese?" she would not reply. If Gauri asked, "Should we go out?" she would grunt and stare at the computer, leaving her decision a mystery until the very last moment, when Anita and Gauri were standing by the door with their shoes on. Outside the apartment, Sahana became a different person, cooing over small dogs, easily flirting with the young cashier at Safeway when she bought a pack of bubble gum, curiously asking the waiter at the Chinese restaurant how many chicken dumplings they made each day.

At the end of that visit, on the way to the airport, Gauri said, "I hope you will be back soon. Your dad says you are both busy these days."

It had not been an accusation, but Sahana took it as one.

"Dad doesn't keep us away. We just don't like it here anymore," she said.

"I'm sorry I can't afford a nicer place," Gauri said, blinking as she looked at the road ahead. "California is expensive."

Anita turned around from the front seat and grimaced at her sister. Sahana looked out the window. Gauri could see her through the rearview mirror. "You're the one who left," Sahana muttered. "You could come back if you wanted to."

Gauri had thought about returning to Pullman many times. The idea of returning as a woman abandoned, by not one but two men, gave her pause. But what really stopped her, prevented her from looking for a job in Pullman, was imagining what her return might do to the girls. Their broken family would be on display for all of Pullman's Indian community to see and talk about, for all of Pullman to judge. Bringing that upon Anita and Sahana was more than she could bear.

"Shut up, Sahana," Anita said. "I'm sure we'll see you soon, Mom."

At the reception, Gauri sits at the family table with Kamal, Sahana, and Christine, who has not changed out of her yellow dress. Samuel's mother, his uncle Peter, and his aunt Terri sit on the other side of the table. Gauri had seen the potbellied, bearded uncle and his pale wife at the morning wedding. Now she learns that Uncle Peter is a schoolteacher from Rhode Island. "Never would have thought I'd visit a place smaller than Narragansett," he says. "But here I am. I'm so happy for these kids."

Aunt Terri, who looks uncomfortable and does not talk much, sips from her water glass too frequently. She is a mural artist, Uncle Peter says. Then he whispers, "She's five years sober."

"Nice dress," Terri says in Gauri's direction, though she does not quite make eye contact when she says it.

"Thank you."

After Anita and Samuel make their entrance into the hall, Kamal rises for the father-daughter dance. Gauri sees

Christine squeeze his hand under the table, just before he stands up. Samuel wheels his mother away. The DJ puts on a slow song that Gauri does not recognize. Kamal keeps one hand on Anita's waist, and watches his feet as he moves. Gauri is happy to see that Anita has worn Indian clothes for the reception, a bright purple ghagra choli. The heavy skirt is covered with gold embroidery and reveals only a hint of her painted toenails. Kamal was not a dancer, but Gauri is impressed by how deliberate he is, by how hard he is trying not to step on Anita's long skirt. He must have practiced.

Less carefully, but gracefully, Samuel dances with his mother. He stands in front of her and holds the handles of her wheelchair. Their eyes are locked as he sways around the dance floor with the chair.

Father and daughter. Mother and son. Gauri watches them, entranced and jealous. There is no place for her here. Her place is with Samuel's father, the long-dead shoe salesman.

By ten o'clock, most of the older guests start leaving. The bride and groom's friends are still dancing. Sahana has been a fixture on the dance floor all night, but Gauri has stayed seated most of the evening, after making one round to say hello to the guests that she knows. There are a few faces that she recognizes: old neighbors, Anita's childhood friends, some Indian families from the early days. When she gets up to get water from the bar, Kamal comes up behind her. He touches her shoulder with four fingers, and again she swallows at his touch, finds herself tensing. She knows his smell so well, a mixture of coconut oil in his hair and Old Spice on his face.

"Amazing, aren't they? The couple?" he says. "Both of our daughters have turned out well."

Gauri nods and softens, moved by his direct acknowledgment of what they made together. For a moment, she feels released from the resentment she felt earlier—when he was dancing with Anita, and when Geetha praised him for organizing the wedding and raising the girls—he had not done it to show off, she thought. He had done it out of love.

"Christine is nice," Gauri says. "I am happy you have found someone."

"It is still new," he says. "But I am happy."

Then he is reticent. A wall is up. She knows that he will not offer more details about Christine. Just like Anita was secretive about Samuel. Just like Sahana is protective about everything.

"Is she the first one?"

He looks at her and his head tips forward a little bit. She sees the surprise on his face, in his eyes. He did not know that she still cared.

He gives her the right answer.

"Yes," he says.

•

When she returns to her table with a glass of water she finds Uncle Peter and Christine deep in conversation.

"Hi there," Peter says to Gauri, his cheeks rosy from drinking. "I was just talking to Christine here about the Costa Rica buddymoon."

"What is a buddymoon?" Gauri asks. She had read about Samuel and Anita's honeymoon on the wedding website. They were going to Belize. There was no mention of anything else.

Peter keeps talking, unaware that Gauri has spoken. "I found it odd, this buddymoon. But Samuel says people do it these days," he says. "Now, inviting your old uncle to go on a beach vacation after your wedding is not something *I* would have done."

"I didn't think Anita would invite us," Christine says, laughing. Christine had read about buddymoons at the dentist's office, in an article in *People* magazine. They were popular in Hollywood. Apparently Jennifer Aniston had one. "A peculiar thing for sure," Christine says.

Gauri is silent. Christine looks at her.

"So you and Kamal are coming," Uncle Peter says to Christine. "It'll be nice for us all to spend some quality time together."

Christine shakes her head, as if she means no. But out loud, she says, "Yes."

"Of course, you will, too?" Peter asks Gauri.

The DJ says something, his voice booming, his words

incomprehensible to Gauri even as they fill her ears. "I can't make it," she says to Peter.

"Too bad. Work keeping you away? What is it that you do, again?"

It is Christine who steps in to save Gauri. "I love this song. You two should dance," she says to Peter and Terri.

Terri shakes her head.

Peter fumbles with his glass, then sets it down.

"Oh, come on," he says. "Have some fun. It's a wedding."

"Thank you," Gauri whispers to Christine.

Gauri does not drink alcohol, she never has, but she suddenly feels lightheaded and daring, the way the remaining guests must be feeling. She hates them all. Those who aren't dancing are milling around the reception hall, drinking "Anitinis" and "Sam and Tonics"—the featured cocktails of the evening—and making small talk, all smiles and chuckles. There had been no alcohol at Gauri and Kamal's wedding, thirty-five years ago in a muggy hall in Erode, no air-conditioning. Just water and filter coffee, served in stainless-steel tumblers.

Gauri walks up to Anita, who is standing alone for the first time all evening, watching the others dance. The DJ is playing a Hindi film song with a fast beat. Anita's black hair is curled and pinned up. Tendrils grace her forehead and cheeks. She had looked beautiful in the morning, during the wedding, but now her makeup is too thickly applied, and to the wrong places. Her blush is too pink, her lipstick too red.

"Who was your makeup lady?" Gauri asks, unable to help herself. There was too little competition in Pullman.

"What?" Anita says, her eyes full of worry. "Is something wrong with my makeup?"

"You aren't wearing the earrings anymore."

"They didn't match."

Just then, Sahana appears, out of breath from dancing, the armpits of her maroon gaghra choli damp circles of sweat. Her gold bangles are miniature chimes when she puts her arm around Anita's waist.

"You invited her and not me?" Gauri asks. She nods towards Christine. "To the buddymoon? Did you think I would not find out? I thought you were going to Belize."

"Oh," Anita says. She looks at Sahana.

"They *are* going to Belize. Afterwards," Sahana says. "We thought Costa Rica would be too expensive for you."

"Is that what Dad said?'

"No," Sahana says.

Gauri looks at Sahana. "Was this your doing?" She did not mean to accuse, did not mean to sound bitter. But it came out that way.

"It was me," Anita says. Her eyes well up. "It was me."

Sahana glares at Gauri and then says brightly, "You could

still come, Mom. There's still time to buy a ticket. We leave in two days."

Sahana takes her arm off Anita's waist, and puts it around Gauri's.

Then she waves at two of Samuel's friends, both tall men in suits, and they walk over.

"Now?" one of the men asks.

"Yes," Sahana says. She kisses Anita's forehead and gives her a gentle push their way.

"Excuse us," the other man says to Gauri. The two of them lift Anita onto their shoulders and parade to the middle of the dance floor. Two other men lift Samuel and a cheering circle forms around the elevated couple.

Sahana turns to Gauri. "You must be tired, Mom," she says. "You should get some rest."

After she leaves the reception, Gauri drives down Main Street, and turns left on South Grand. The drive to the hotel is less than ten minutes. There is an even shorter way, but she chooses this one. She recalls driving these roads every day when the girls were young, to get to preschool, music classes, the grocery store, doctor appointments. Every summer, during the annual Lentil Festival, Gauri, Kamal, and the girls walked from Military Hill to downtown to watch the parade.

The memory of the past, the futility of the future, it leaves her breathless. She opens the car windows to let cool air in. She will look for tickets to Costa Rica. Yes, she thinks, I will stay in Pullman for two extra days with Geetha and Bhaskar, and then go to the buddymoon.

But by the time she reaches the hotel, she feels the impossibility of it. A ticket to Costa Rica is more than she can afford. Even the ticket from San Francisco to Seattle had been too much. The rental car, the gas. All too much. She is grateful to Kamal for paying for the room. It is a kindness she will remember.

In the hotel bathroom, she peels her dress off her body. It sits in a clump on the tile floor. She will never wear it again. From her suitcase, she retrieves a pink cotton nightie dotted with white flowers and slips it on. She sees the wedding invitation in the suitcase and picks it up. "Anita and Samuel," it says. An invitation to brunch the following day, at the Garden House Café, is printed on it. She drops it in the trash, takes a jar of moisturizer out of her suitcase, and rubs cream into her legs and arms. She has aged well but still, her skin is lightly spotted, looser than it once was. In bed, as her eyelids grow heavy, she falls asleep feeling like an old woman.

The next day, as she drives back to Seattle, it occurs to her that the wedding must have cost thousands of dollars. Tens of thousands. She is seized with anger. The wedding, the reception, the brunch she has chosen not to attend, all of it was so expensive.

Gauri wonders whether Samuel's mother was invited to Costa Rica. Simply from the way Samuel had looked at her, the tenderness with which he'd held the handlebars of her wheelchair, Gauri is sure that she was.

In Ellensburg, she passes an antique store painted a greenish blue and the color reminds her of the robin and its eggs. When the girls were in preschool, a robin once made a nest on their windowsill. She and Kamal and the girls waited for weeks for the bird's brightly colored eggs to hatch.

Gauri loosens her grip on the steering wheel. She cannot be tenacious and desperate. It was her fault for leaving Pullman, her fault for not coming back. Now she had to be yielding, and in the slack, she and the girls, maybe even she and Kamal, would find an ease. Things will be different, she tells herself. She would call more often, send better presents. Perhaps there would be grandchildren to spoil, in the future.

When the eggs finally hatched, the whole family had watched, awestruck. The baby birds each had a layer of translucent pink skin draped over their bulging eyeballs, blind at birth. The mother bird crowded the nest, dropped food into each tiny beak. How many days did it take before they opened their eyes? The fields of Eastern Washington blur past the window, as Gauri tries to recall.

Amma

Before all of this, before they prostrated at her feet, before she wore large, round, dark red bottus with light red namams on her forehead, she was one of us. Before she became chief minister, before she became a star, she was our classmate at Sacred Heart Girls School in Church Park. "We knew her before it all started," we still like to say. She was Jaya.

We know the stories. One artist used five liters of his own blood, frozen, to make a life-size sculpture of her head. A police superintendent cut his fingertips off and delivered them to the Ganesh temple, praying, "May my sacrifice result in her reelection." A martial arts teacher asked his students to drive nails through his hands and feet, made a speech in praise of her, and then fainted. When she saw the video, she wrote the teacher a handwritten letter. "Please never do that again." He touched the letter to his cheek and framed it.

She appeals to the fisherman, the rickshaw driver, the bricklayer. Her devotees are of all types: children, women,

men. So many men. They consider her beyond human, a shimmering goddess, their heroine, indestructible.

We know who she became. She was the greatest actress of her time, mistress to the biggest Kollywood star of our era, the heroine of twenty-eight of his films. When her beloved quit films and became the chief minister of Tamil Nadu, she, not his wife, was his escort to every convention, every gala, every state dinner. He died. She ran for office. She won. Cinema star, mistress, politician, and amma to an entire state for nearly as long as we had our children in our homes. But we knew her when we were children ourselves.

Sacred Heart Girls School was a pleasant place back then. Sacred Heart was the type of school that fostered equality, beginning with the admissions process. The fees were fair enough, attracting girls from all kinds of families. The nuns who ran the school, wearing pleated white robes and perpetual frowns, were strict but kind, and this pleased our parents. There was a heavy homework load—we read *As You Like It* and memorized Yeats, solved algebra equations, and learned physics. Assignments were carefully graded; test scores at the school were good, and college admissions all but guaranteed.

It wasn't all about studying. During our free period we rolled up the sleeves of our uniform shirts and played badminton, and shrieked when our rackets missed the shuttlecock.

We snickered about our physical education teacher, Prem Sir, who wore sweatpants in spite of the scorching Madras sun, and said, “Hands on hips, now side to side,” as he swayed his body back and forth.

We were at that age when things were beginning to happen—like when Shalini Iyer got tangled up with DaCosta. Shalini was in Standard X at Sacred Heart, and DaCosta went to the boys’ school down the street. He was an Anglo-Indian with a sharp nose and long, thick eyelashes. Every morning, we watched him cycle by our school, trying to catch a glimpse of Shalini. At lunchtime, she would sneak out to meet him.

Most of us in Standard VI watched this with fascination, but did not have romantic interests of our own quite yet. Two of us, many years later, would pursue love marriages, but at that stage we were prepubescent and had little contact with boys who were not our brothers. The first time Shalini was caught, she was sentenced to lunch in the office for a whole month. When she was caught again, she was expelled. It so happened that Jaya arrived that same day that Shalini was expelled from Sacred Heart. It was a Wednesday in mid-August, right after Independence Day. Jaya—the new girl, then—had wide coffee-colored eyes. Her school uniform didn’t fit properly, not for lack of quality tailoring, but because she had *that* sort of body, one with flab and fat that pushed against seams and defied buttons and belts.

Our parents spoke in whispers about Jaya’s family, and

the curious among us collected the gossip: Her father died when she was in nursery school, and left all of his money to his second wife. Her mother was a single woman raising a child, an actress by profession. Not a heroine, but a character actress. In every movie, she played the vixen, a villainous creature that lured the hero away from the leading lady.

Actress.

It had all sorts of connotations.

She worked constantly, and the films paid something, so they had money. Not as much as Srimathi's parents, who owned a jewelry store, but enough. Still, our parents held her in low regard—*She has even shown her bare thigh in a film*, our mothers said in disgust. During her rare school appearances, there was not a parent or nun or teacher who did not look at Jaya's mother. They stared openly at her long cream-colored neck, at her eyes lined with liquid black.

The biggest difference we noticed between Jaya and every other girl at Sacred Heart, rich or not so rich, was that her family never came to school. When her mother came to our Annual Day celebration, Jaya walked onto the school grounds proudly holding her hand. Backstage, she kept saying how happy she was that her mother had the evening off. But then, halfway through the show, her mother left for a shoot and missed our class skit entirely.

Mostly, Jaya was ferried to and fro by household staff. A driver named Rama dropped her off and picked her up, and a teenage servant girl named Rosie delivered a stainless-steel tiffin box every day at noon.

As children, we had none of the preconceived notions that our parents had. We were with Jaya every day, in our classrooms with cold concrete floors and on our sandy playground. We shared our slates with her, and our chalk. We included her in our games. Children are like that. They take care of each other. But children can also be cruel.

Moosarundai Moorthy.

Rotund junk-food eater.

Madhavi started calling her that behind her back. "All in fun," she said. But it stuck. Soon we were all saying it. In truth, Jaya was overfed, not greedy. There is a difference. Every day at lunchtime, the rest of us raced to our tiffin carriers and stuffed whatever our mothers had packed into our mouths. Jaya was not like that. Most of our tiffin carriers had two containers. Hers had four, and she did not begin eating until she carefully took each one out and spread them before her at the lunch table. She never left a morsel uneaten.

Our teacher that year was Chama Miss. She was neither our favorite teacher at Sacred Heart nor the best one, but she was the teacher who had the chocolates. Chama Miss was a graduate of Sacred Heart herself. To teach at the same school you attended was considered a failure by us back then, a sign that you were incapable of moving on. She wore block-print saris in morose shades of brown and gray, which made her rail-thin figure look even less feminine than it was. Her curly hair refused to stay in a neat braid, and strands were always bursting free. Often, we caught her quietly eating tiny bars of Dairy Milk when she thought no one was looking, sometimes early in the day, before the morning bell even rang. Rumor had it that her brother was a cacao researcher for Cadbury's, at their Kerala R&D plant. Among ourselves, we called her "Chocolate Miss," a reference both to her tastes and her complexion.

Chama Miss loved Jaya. When called on in class, Jaya never stumbled on her words like the rest of us. Rather, she wrote down what she wanted to say and then spoke slowly and clearly. Even when her answer was incorrect, Chama Miss was impressed. "Very good, Jaya. Were you all watching?" she would say in her high, girlish voice. "Think. Wait. Then speak."

One day, Jaya approached us to show off her new marbles during recess. Srimathi, busy gossiping with another girl, did not see her and said, "Moosarundai Moorthy. Did you see the size of her lunch today?"

The rest of us froze. Srimathi turned to see Jaya walking away, her marbles heavy and visible in her skirt pocket.

Madhavi shouted, "Ey, Jaya. Take it as a joke."

"Yes," we said. "We were only joking."

Madhavi's twin, Latha, ran after Jaya, but it was too late. She had run into the girls' bathroom and shut the door behind her. She stopped speaking to us. Chama Miss sat with

Jaya every day at lunch after that, and glared at us if we went their way.

We thought we had lost our strange new friend. But a week or so later, things were back to normal. She ate lunch with us and played with us. We, too, acted like nothing had happened.

As she began her acting career, the rest of us were college students, still living with our parents. Eight of us went to Women's Christian College, and we met for lunch daily under the white silk-cotton tree, each of us sitting on one of its thick exposed roots. It was impossible not to talk about her.

She had graduated first in our class, and was offered a full merit scholarship to Stella Maris; not one of us received anything close to such an opportunity. But she took a movie offer instead, and did not even attend convocation. She was slender at the waist by then, with luscious hips, the baby fat completely rearranged. She had pimples, but makeup fixed that. As the class of 1966 walked nervously across the stage to collect our diplomas, her image was already on billboards, kilometers of her midriff visible, her lips half open, her eyes in a sidelong glance towards all the pedestrians of Madras.

Posters of her films were plastered on walls and on wooden signposts. We watched her films with our parents, with our friends, whenever we could spare the three rupees. We tuned in to Radio Ceylon on our crackly transistor radios in the evenings, so we could listen to her songs as we helped our mothers prepare dinner.

She was on Page 3 often, once pictured with her thick black hair in a long braid, clad in a rose-colored Mysore silk sari that sold out at Nalli the week after, wearing gold studs with red gem centers that street peddlers had imitations of within days. Srimathi bought a pair of those imitation earrings. One day at lunch, she pulled them out of her purse to show us. We were surprised, as it was the first we knew of her desire to be like Jaya. She tilted the blue box towards us and we saw the glint of the artificial red gems. She passed the box around but forbade us from touching the earrings. "Price?" we asked. "One hundred rupees," she said. We gasped. "Tacky design, if you ask me," Madhavi said, when it was her turn to look. "No, they are lovely," Latha insisted, always the sunshine to her twin sister's spite.

When you know someone like Jaya—know her from back then, when she was pudgy, and wore a uniform, and two plaits tied with white ribbons, just like you—seeing her on the big screen is different for you than it is for anyone else. You imagine that you are her, and that she is you. You *know* her. You look at her bangs, the curls on her forehead. You watch how she slides her bare arm across a grand piano while her co-star plays with quick-moving fingers. You watch the way she blinks, slowly. The way she dances under a waterfall and gets drenched. How her nipples protrude through her blouse. You wonder how it is that her hair gets wet but her makeup stays intact. You watch her lover put his hand on the wet bare skin of her waist, just above where her sari's inskirt is tied.

When you get home from the theater, you snip your hair, try to curl it with your pencil. Then you slide your arm across the windowsill. Your father walks by, gives you a peculiar look, and says, "God help you." He sees the college textbook you have open, its pages unmarked and unread. "I hope you pass biology."

Before you take off your clothes to bathe, you take a mugful of cold water, pour it over yourself, and then look down at your body, at your own erect nipples protruding through your sari blouse. Then you add hot water to the bucket so you can take a bath. Only then do you take your clothes off, wring the water out of them. You put your own hand on your own bare skin, right where it curves inward, just above the hip joint. You imagine you are her. You do this and you are young, like Jaya. You do not know that you will do this again much later, when you are old and she is in jail, when your waist is no longer as firm and small and arched as it once was.

•

We were married, every one of us, by the age of twenty-three, college degrees secured or not. Almost all of us had children. Radha was unable to conceive; we had our doubts about her husband from the moment we saw him at the wedding. Hema, who loved children, had miscarriage after miscarriage and then went crazy and stopped speaking to us. Eventually she stopped speaking altogether.

We did not gather in those days. There was no time. No time, even, to write or post letters. But we watched her films. All her films. She played us in her films. A woman with a philandering husband, a housewife with children, a housewife without children, a mentally unstable woman, a philandering woman. Other times, she played people we could only imagine: an island princess, an undercover CBI agent.

She lived in a bungalow called Poes Garden, not too far from Sacred Heart. It was a boxy, modern mystery of a house, with a garden full of green grass, soft and lush, as if she lived in England or America. We ran our fingers through bags of long-grain rice, through steel drums filled with dry pigeon peas, and imagined that the sensation of walking barefoot through that grass was something similar, a cool tickle that traveled upwards through the body. We imagined her dressed in shimmery salwars and sheer saris, sipping on frothy drinks with her co-star and lover. Hema, our poor, silent, childless Hema, saw Jaya once at

Jaffar's on Mount Road, eating peach Melba with her lover. Jaya spoke to her. "Sacred Heart. Yes, of course I remember. How are you?" Hema broke her silence for a moment to report the news to Srimathi. "She remembered me," Hema said, on the phone.

We needed to see Jaya that way, glamorous and desirable, and still human. We were in that stage of life and motherhood that is filled with fatigue, unimaginable to the young, forgotten by the old, unknown altogether to those without children. We spent our days washing tiny bottoms, wiping hot, fresh vomit off the floors, pulling wooden combs through knotty hair. Picking lice. Unclogging nostrils. We shouted often. "Brush your teeth! Take a bath! Pack your books!"

We poured idli and dosa batter with urgency, desperate to feed our children before we pushed them out the door. We filled water bottles and tied shoelaces. Two o'clock came too soon, and then we had to prepare a snack, and keep milk ready, and make fresh tiffins for the evening. Some of us had help. Some of us had more of it than others. Madhavi married rich. She was the better-looking twin. She had a housekeeper and a cook, but even that was so much work, she said. "Management is a full-time job," she liked to say.

At night, when our aching backs searched for comfortable positions on our stiff, cotton-stuffed mattresses, we imagined that Jaya's bedroom was like a suite in a grand Taj hotel. We uttered these thoughts to our husbands in the dead of the night, our sleeping children sandwiched in our bed.

"Someone must massage her feet with expensive lotion."

"Her tea appears at her bedside."

"She has no children who tug on her pallu every five minutes."

Our husbands, tired and groggy from their long days at work, did not entertain our fantasies about her, though perhaps they had their own.

"Sounds nice," they said, before turning their bodies away from us, leaving us wide-eyed and staring at the ceiling.

"The loneliness must kill her," we whispered to ourselves, as the ceiling fans above us swung around and around. With each turn of the fan, we saw her smiling face. Her scheming wink. A madwoman, a secretary, a village belle.

It takes a decade, or maybe two, but eventually, you no longer wish to be her. You no longer want her to be you. You are happy being yourself, or resigned, or too afraid to be anyone but yourself. When you see her on the billboards, or on the television that you now own, you feel sorry for her. You have a daughter and a husband. Or you are a widow, but at least you have a son. Perhaps your husband has a mistress, but at least he spends half his time with you. Or you have no children, and you cannot speak, but you have a small home, and you love the man who lives in it, and he loves you.

Her lover is dead. He never once publicly acknowledged

their relationship. At his funeral, when his body was being carried through the streets, she walked alongside his head, a clear insult to his wife, who was by his feet. His nephew told Jaya to move. When she did not, he pushed her, and she fell. We saw it all on live television. Her real life, a tragic film of its own. She was a star, but she had no idea what it was like to have a sleeping baby's hand grip her finger for hours at a time. She did not know the feeling of opening the door each afternoon to beautiful children holding brown cloth book bags, their stray hairs sweaty and sticky against their foreheads.

The year that Jaya turned forty—we *all* turned forty—she became chief minister, and had to morph her image from coy actress to shrewd politician. From a pretty woman every man wanted, to a powerful woman they respected. "Call me sister," she said in interviews.

She started to wear heavy green silk saris and her trademark red bottu. No more embroidered chiffon. No more sheer Georgette. She was often photographed with her palms together in a vannakam, or with her right-hand index and middle fingers raised high above her to indicate two leaves on a stem, the emblem of her party. When we made fun of Srimathi for hanging a picture of Jaya on her wall, as if Jaya were part of her family, she was defensive.

"She is in charge of our entire state, after all."

Once again, Jaya's image was all over Tamil Nadu. On billboards, and across the sides of buildings. But now, when full-bladdered men saw her face in front of theirs, they pulled their pant zips back up and hurried to a different wall.

Jaya traveled around the state in a white Ambassador. A caravan of identical Ambassadors drove ahead of and behind her, so that ill-wishers were kept guessing. When traffic was blocked in Madras, our children peered out of our cars, or the rickshaw, or the city bus, and said, "Must be because of Aunty." They called her Aunty because we told them to. From the time they were babies, we had pointed her image out to them. *That's our friend*, we said. *There's Aunty*, we said. Never mind that none of our children had ever seen her in person. Since our school days, nor had we.

Yes, we turned forty as Jaya did. We were her classmates, after all, aging at the same pace. We were not famous or powerful, but with our children in high school, our time began to free up. We started our monthly teas, always in Srimathi's flat in Annanagar because it was centrally located. Her drawing room had enough seating for us all, and she did not mind preparing a few snacks.

It was our only true break and we relished it. We no longer had nappies to deal with, or tantrums of the fist-pounding sort, there was less vomit, but still, life was no vacation. Our work was constant. And yet, when we met for tea, we spoke proudly of our beautiful children, laughed about our silly husbands, and bragged about the details of our quiet but fulfilling lives. And of course, we spoke of Jaya.

Srimathi owned the original records from all of Jaya's films, and while we played them on her Jensen turntable, one after another, we fretted.

"Poor girl," we said, as we looked at Jaya's photo, which hung above Srimathi's television set. "What is a life without a family?

"She must not know what to do with her time in the evenings," Srimathi said.

"She is chief minister. She must have many duties," Latha said. She lived in Bangalore but she visited Madras sometimes, and joined our teas when she could.

"She has professional duties, not personal ones. There is a distinction," Madhavi said, sharp-tongued as ever.

"And the weight she is putting on these days."

"Predisposed, poor thing. Don't you remember?"

She *was* a plump child. We all remembered.

Once we started our Sunday afternoon teas, we continued them with regularity, and relied on them as everything changed around us: our children grew up, took jobs, married, and became young mothers and fathers themselves. During her second term as chief minister, Jaya further recast her image, elevating herself to the highest pedestal.

"Call me Amma," she said. *Mother.* As if to say, "You are all my children."

"She is really acting in her own film now," Madhavi said.

We read her dramas in the papers. Her brother and his family lived with her for a time, but she alienated them with her eccentric behavior, at one point adopting a grown man as a son. Rumor was she decorated a room full of soft toys for this man, as if he were a small boy. Disgusted, her brother and his family left. Eventually, Jaya told the adopted son to leave. We gawked at the picture of him walking out of Poes Garden, his head hanging in shame, his arms full of stuffed bears and bunnies.

"She can't seem to keep a friend," we said. "Does she like being alone?"

"Yet how is it," Latha mused, "that in a man's world, she alone knows how to control men? How does she make them stop and listen?"

After two successful terms, Jaya lost an election. Her rival was her dead lover's onetime friend and longtime enemy, a man who was also from the film industry, a former screenwriter. After this bitter loss, she isolated herself completely. Every evening, she retreated into Poes Garden. The windows were always shut. She lost contact with her family. She made a secret trip to America to insert a gastric sleeve, and an unauthorized photo of her on the operating table appeared in a gossip rag.

"Poor Jaya," we said. "If only she had stayed in touch. We could help her."

But the year we all turned fifty, a surprise: the papers reported that Hema, our childless, silent Hema, and Hema's husband had moved into Poes Garden with Jaya.

"They are my dearest friends, and my managers," Jaya told the press. By this time, she had a thick, well-built double chin that moved up and down when she spoke. "Without them, nothing would get done."

We had no idea that Hema had been talking to Jaya through the years. We had no idea Hema was talking at all. "How did it start," we wanted to ask Hema, and more important, "Is there any of the girl we knew left?" But we had no way of reaching Hema at Poes Garden.

Then Jaya kicked Hema's husband out. Immediately, rumors began circulating. There was an article about Jaya and Hema in *Starfare*. A grainy image of two women with linked hands, cheeks pressed to each other. *Childhood friends a little too close*, the caption read. But after that, she told Hema to get out too.

"She cannot seem to keep a friend," we said, once again.

When she ran for reelection once more, her supporters did everything they could to help. In Kanchipuram, 2,001 men broke coconuts over their heads for Amma. In Tiruppur, 3,050 of her followers marched along the Noyyal River with urns of milk on their heads. In Madurai, 634 women lit oil lamps. The numbers were all exact, numbers her astrologer said were auspicious for her.

To buy the votes of the poor, her party created a welfare program, and distributed goods branded with her name and image to millions. Amma salt, Amma sugar, Amma pencil boxes, Amma food processors. Amma-subsidized laptops. Free underwear. Free undershirts. Free sanitary napkins.

She won.

Now the papers were full of praise for her work as chief minister. Midday meals for the poor at Amma canteens, Amma medical clinics. Our humble mother. Our amma. Voice of the party. Savior of the Ordinary Tamilian. Once a heroine, now a superwoman. She started wearing a shawl around her shoulders, a cape over her green silk saris. The shawls were always green. Always silk. Always heavy. Under the saris, some say, she wore a bulletproof vest.

The time between childhood and old age passes quickly, leaving you feeling like your entire life is a double feature with no intermission. You wake up one day, look in the mirror, and wonder who you are, and where everyone is. Your body does not feel old, not yet. But your hair is half gray. Maybe you dye it. Maybe you let it be. Either way, it is thin now. Your children have left. Your husband is dead. Or your husband is alive but when you pretend to look away, you no longer catch him admiring you. He is always irritable. He never wants to go on holiday. You meet your friends for tea, and when you do, you see how old they look and finally admit that you, too, must look like them. They do not empathize with your worries, because they have worse problems, darker secrets (a drinking habit, a husband with a drinking habit, a husband who does not like women, an abusive mother-in-law, an estranged child). "You will get through it," they say, half-heartedly.

You go home and look in the mirror again. Now you feel it, the oldness of you.

Chama Miss showed us the chocolate in the morning, dozens of bars the size of our heads. It was the last day of school before the Diwali holidays during our Standard VI year, so she brought bars of Cadbury's for all twenty-six of us. Perhaps her brother, the cacao researcher, had given them to her, we whispered as we eyed the treats. Then Chama Miss put the chocolate bars away, saying she would distribute them at the end of the day.

"We have work to do," she said. She tucked the pallu of her sari in at her hip and clapped her hands. "Time for civics. Bring out your books."

She turned to the board and wrote "Ambedkar."

"Who was he?" she asked, turning back around to face us.

"Founding father, Miss," Jaya said.

"Does anyone know what Ambedkar believed in?"

"Liberty, equality, fraternity," Madhavi said. Then she snickered.

The rest of us were fixated on Chama Miss's bag, where she had stashed the bars of chocolates. We thought of how the sugary blocks would dissolve in our mouths, leaving us with nuts and fruits to bite and chew. Wouldn't the bars melt? Why wasn't she handing them out now?

None of us can say who was responsible for what happened next.

At recess, we found ourselves in the alley towards the back of the school, where the restrooms were. This was the sandy strip that all the teachers avoided because of the toilet smell. Twenty-six of us stood there, with twenty-six bars of chocolate. We ate them ferociously. Jaya too. The chocolate had indeed melted, so we licked the foil clean. We chewed the fruits and bit the nuts. Then we gathered all the wrappers into a large pile. We wiped the gooey remnants off our faces with handkerchiefs. There were five minutes to spare before class started, and we had to act quickly.

"Jaya, will you hide the wrappers in the empty storage room next to the science laboratory?" we asked. "Go now."

"Why me?"

"We need your help. Chama Miss likes you. She will not mind if you walk into class late."

Jaya stood up, gathered the wrappers, and walked towards the storage room.

We were all in our seats when the bell rang. All but one.

At first, Chama Miss did not notice. But when she asked us for the answers to our math sums, she paused. Usually, Jaya raised her hand.

"Where is she?" Chama Miss asked, panic rising in her voice.

"She went home at lunch," we said.

"She was not sick this morning."

"She was sick at lunch."

We moved on to other lessons. At the end of the day, Chama Miss searched her bag for the missing chocolates.

"Where are they?" she asked the class. "I want to distribute them."

No one answered.

"Where are the chocolates?" she said again, louder this time. She hit her wooden pointer against her desk. Her gaze shifted from student to student.

"She ate them."

"Who?"

"Jaya."

"All of them? All twenty-six of them?"

"All of them."

"Each of you," Chama Miss said, "will be going home with notes. Unless you tell me what happened."

"We saw her go towards the storeroom," Latha, the sweet twin, said quietly. Then she burst into tears.

Chama Miss walked briskly to the storeroom, all of us in tow. It was locked with a padlock from the outside. She used her key to open it, and found Jaya lying in the center of the room on the floor, curled in a ball, chocolate streaked across her face. She was silent, and her eyes were puffy. A single purple wrapper, its aluminum backside twinkling from the sunlight that shone through the open door, was by her feet. The rest of the pile, a mound of twenty-five wrappers, was a bit farther away.

"Who locked her in this room?" Chama Miss demanded.

"Not me."

"Not me."

"Not me."

"Did you eat the chocolates?" she asked Jaya.

"Miss. I ate them," she said. Her voice was raspy, perhaps from crying, perhaps from shouting for help. "Sorry, Miss."

"All of them?"

"All of them."

"Are you sure?"

"Yes."

"Then I must suspend you."

We spent a long Diwali holiday thinking about what

happened. We were sure that Jaya would hate us. "She will never speak to us again," we said.

Ten days later, back at school, it was as if the whole incident had been forgotten. She answered when we called her to join our games, or to eat lunch with us. She smiled at us. She offered her help with reading and sums when we were struggling. But something was different this time. The eagerness was gone, that enthusiasm she'd had, to jostle us and tell us jokes, to show off her new toys, or giggle with us when Prem Sir shook his hips.

If we did not call her to our side, she sat by herself or with one of the teachers, or with the younger girls. It was not that she seemed lonely, only that she preferred to be alone. Eventually, instead of lunch, she had just two bananas. The pounds slipped off and by Standard XII she became that woman all of Tamil Nadu came to know, the one with incredible proportions.

"She has a consultant who monitors her diet and workouts," our mothers said. "They spend a fortune on it. But acting is a family business, so what else can they do? Good thing she ate her fill when she was younger."

"She's the best student among us," we told our mothers. But our mothers did not listen. They believed what they wanted to believe.

•

When the news arrives, you rush back to your friends. Finally, you have something to talk about.

The police took her away in the morning, right from Poes Garden. They found 10,500 saris, 14 exotic birds, 850 pairs of shoes, an entire bedroom set made of silver—a bed frame, a nightstand, and drawers—and 94 pounds of gold hidden in a secret vault, buried under her green grass. Total cash assets that could not be accounted for from her films or her state salary: 700 million rupees.

"I knew it all along," Madhavi says. She shrugs. "I just could not say." Her husband is the inspector general of police.

"You did not even hint of this to me," her sister, Latha, says skeptically.

"I could not." Madhavi sniffs. "It was top secret."

You did not know. Not at all. This disturbs you deeply, that you knew Jaya for so long and had no idea what she was capable of.

Messages fly back and forth between you and your friends for weeks on the Sacred Heart Whatsapp group. What would happen to Amma? What would happen to the house? She was put under house arrest while the judge deliberated.

Srimathi finds an old picture in her bureau. Standard VI. 1960. Sacred Heart Girls Matriculation School. Chama Miss is in the photo, rail thin. You are in it. She is in it.

Somehow, the photo ends up on the news. A reporter calls.

“Can you tell us what she was like? Can you share anything?”

You hold the phone and do not speak.

“Please, Madam. Anything at all? What did she like to eat?”

You hang up.

The phone rings again. This time it is a police investigator.

“Madam, we need to speak to you. We are following all leads. Any small thing you can remember?”

“No,” you say. “It was so long ago. Nothing to do with now.”

“If you think of anything, please call,” the investigator says politely, before hanging up.

You hear sirens. Outside your flat window, you see flashing lights. You look down, and your hands are cuffed. An officer with a thick mustache is looking at you with hatred in his eyes. We were very young, you want to say. It was just chocolate. But all that comes out is “Can I use the loo before we leave?” He gives you a wide grin, as if you are a child still. You are going to die, you know it. Then you feel a hand on your arm, shaking you. It is your husband. “Wake up,” he says. “You are having a bad dream. Your pillow is soaked with sweat.”

The day that she was acquitted, we watched it on television. Thousands of people stood in front of Poes Garden, where she was under house arrest. They were waiting for her to come out and thank her well-wishers. We knew she would come. We kept the television on for hours. People danced on the streets. Some wore paper masks with her face on it. Srimathi was there. The camera panned across her face. She was wearing those earrings. Amma's devotees brought garlands of marigold, and after dark, they lit sparklers that they circled around in the air. The paramedics came twice. First when an old man collapsed on the street from exhaustion. Then again when a woman went into labor and gave birth. It was evening. Then eleven. Then midnight. We kept watching. She did not appear. Word finally came; it was not an auspicious day or time for her to present herself in public. Her astrologer wanted her to wait until morning. But the crowd stayed. Someone set up a speaker system on the streets. They danced all night to her old film songs. We stayed up with them, though we did not dance. At last, at dawn, she emerged wearing a green silk sari. Her green shawl was wrapped around her shoulders. She brought her palms together and bowed. Vannakam. Then the camera zoomed in and we saw it. We saw all of it at once. We were the only ones who could. Amma, the overweight politician, cunning and double-chinned. The famous actress, voluptuous and doe-eyed. And Jaya, the girl who played with marbles and loved chocolates, as any child would.

Nature Exchange

Behind the tennis courts, Veena finds the grassy clearing that has been fruitful for her. Since her move to the area a week and a half ago, she has found a dead monarch with its wings intact, and half a mouse skull.

Today, she has less luck. She picks up a handful of green-capped acorns and two pine cones. Then she spots something shiny in the grass. An iridescent abalone shell, surely dropped by a child who brought it back from a beach vacation in Florida or California.

"Hi."

She turns to find a boy, hardly four years in age, standing behind her. He has bright eyes. Brown eyes.

"What are you doing?" he asks. A sweatband made of blue terry cloth keeps his long blond hair out of his eyes.

A woman, her figure flat as a pancake, stands at his side.

"Sorry," she says to Veena. The woman raises her eyebrows and offers Veena a knowing smile, at once both apologetic and proud. "He likes to talk."

"I dropped something," Veena says to the boy.

"I can help you find it," the boy says. "I'm good at finding things."

She thinks about giving him the shell. It is in her right fist, its edges pressed against her palm. With her other hand she massages her side. She has an ache in her hip that she notices only when she stops moving.

Finders, keepers, a voice in her head says.

"No, you can't," she says out loud. She massages her hip again. The boy watches her do this.

His mother takes hold of his hand.

"We should go," she says. "Finish our walk and let this nice lady finish hers."

The boy persists even after Veena turns to leave.

"What did you lose?"

Veena puts the morning's haul into the tote hanging from the doorknob of her bedroom, a room she has all to herself. The tote contains a portion of her son Neel's collection. The rest is still in her moving boxes. Before she and Mitchell separated, it had hung from their bedroom door and he frequently complained that it was too heavy, that the knob would fall off. But he never made her move it.

The last time they took Neel to the nature center was on

a Sunday, two weeks before he died. Two years ago now. He was seven. The exchange is a single large room near the nature center's entrance, a place where children can bring in found natural objects and trade them in for points towards prizes, all from nature. The shelves have bins and drawers and everything is neatly categorized. There are lotus pods, sand dollars, barnacles, sea beans, devil's claws. Bark, pine cones, paper wasp nests. Dead, dried-up insects: butterflies, beetles, grasshoppers, earwigs, houseflies. Tiny pins with slips of paper pierce insect bodies, identifying them by scientific name. *Dermaptera. Musca domestica. Caelifera.* Some items are local, others are most certainly ordered in bulk from a wholesaler.

Everything has a price in points.

Small, standard shells such as scallops, clams, and cockles cost twenty points. Shark-eye shells are twenty-five. Big or unusual shells cost up to two hundred apiece. A large conch, of which there is only one on display at a time, is one thousand. Little polished stones, fifty. Small geodes, five hundred. Mid-sized geodes, two thousand. Big geodes, four thousand. And the elk antlers, up on the highest shelf in the back corner of the room, unreachable by any human under seven feet tall without aid of a step stool, are ten thousand points. They are gleaming and polished, each side with four spiky branches. A donation from a hunting family that loves nature.

"The young man with his eye on the antlers," the white-haired woman behind the desk said when Neel walked in on that final Sunday. The woman's name was Rosemary.

She looked at Veena and Mitchell. "I love him," she mouthed, her lips, colored raspberry, moving deliberately. She wore a seashell-patterned blouse. She was typical of the center's employees: patient, older, a lover of nature, eager to share that love with the next generation. She was always there on Sundays, and Veena knew her blouses well—the one with planets, the one with dinosaurs, the one with microscopic organisms, the one with mammals of the savanna.

Neel surveyed all the objects in the room, moving from shelf to shelf. He opened drawers, ran his small fingers across the edge of a prickly pine cone, peered through the mouth of a sand dollar with one eye. He blew air up towards the strands of hair that fell across his eyes. He needed a haircut.

Then, abruptly, wordlessly, the moment marked, as always, by a satisfied sigh, he was done. He took his canvas bag to Rosemary, and carefully placed his three rocks for trade on the desk, leaving a gap between each one. Up to three items could be traded in per day.

He watched as Rosemary picked up the rock with lustrous flakes.

"Tell me about it," she said.

Neel took a small notebook out of his bag and flipped through it until he found what he was looking for. The notebook itself had little written in it, just a drawing and a word or two, but his oral report was thorough.

"A gift from Toby, found in his grandmother's backyard. Likely to be igneous with mica."

Rosemary nodded. "I believe you're right."

When she set it down in a different spot, Neel moved it back to where he had first set it.

"Sorry," Rosemary said. Veena could hear the kindness in her voice. She understood Neel. So many people did not.

Rosemary picked up another rock. "And this?"

"Discovered last Friday at four p.m. in my backyard. Fossil seashell. Cretaceous."

"A mold, isn't it?"

"Of course," Neel said. "Not a cast."

Rosemary leaned in.

Still holding the fossil mold, she pointed to the third rock.

"Parking lot of Publix, while Mommy was putting groceries in the car. Ordinary gravel, but shaped like a blue whale."

"Wonder can be as ordinary as a piece of gravel," Rosemary said.

For Rosemary, the questions were protocol. The mission of the exchange was to help children observe the natural world around them, to be curious and respectful, and also have fun. Asking questions was also a way for her to confirm that they did not disrupt anything alive in their pursuit.

"All nonliving today, Neel?"

A simple question, but Neel had a long answer. He explained the scientific definition of nonliving: things that cannot grow, move or breathe. And of the living: anything that has ever needed food and water and produced waste.

Rosemary's eyes did not glaze over when Neel spoke. There was no smirk. Instead, she looked at Veena and seemed to silently acknowledge Neel's brilliance.

"So, a dead thing is living," Neel concluded. "Because it was once alive."

"That's right. Let's add it up, shall we?" she said.

Neel moved close to Rosemary as she input his points, as if supervising her work. He did not understand the concept of personal space, according to the school counselor who was trying to help him with it.

"Move back," Veena said. He was so close that Rosemary could probably feel his warm breath on her neck.

"He's fine," Rosemary said.

Neel spent a few of his points on an extra-large sand dollar, a polished tiger's eye with silky shades of yellow and brown, and a white wolf tooth shaped like a crescent moon. He was always careful not to spend too much.

"What's my current total?" he asked.

"After today's purchases, you're at three thousand, four hundred and ninety-eight," Rosemary said.

"Still a lot left to go," he said.

After the visit to the exchange, Veena, Mitchell, and Neel had plans to visit Veena's parents, who lived farther north, in Roswell. But first, they went to Taco Planet, for a late breakfast, the three of them each ordering the same migas tacos.

"Do we have to go to Ammamma and Thatha's house today?" Neel asked. "I wanted to play with Toby."

"You can play with Toby tomorrow," Veena said. "You know, I only met my grandparents a few times. We didn't go to India often."

"I know," Neel said. Mitchell patted his back.

"You're lucky we live so close to them," Veena said.

"So lucky," Neel said. He rolled his eyes. He had just started doing that.

In the shower, hot water streams over Veena's body and she turns the handle to make it hotter, allowing the jets to scald her back.

She wanted to make time for the nature center today. The daily three-item limit meant it was important that she went frequently. If Mitchell helped, if he added points to Neel's account too, it would be so much easier. But he would not help.

"Veena," he said, when she told him the address of the house she was moving into, how close it was to the center. "You need to stop."

For the first two months after Neel died, Veena and

Mitchell had sex every night, starting from the night Neel's body was taken to the morgue at Emory University Hospital. It was she who sought him out under the cool sheets, wrapping her arms around his shoulders, tearless but full of sorrow, hopeful that she could lose herself in his hair and scent. Everything else was impossible—walking, smiling, opening mail, eating—but the sex was addictive, a temporary relief, as dismal as it was necessary.

Then, after those two months, it stopped—the relief, the need, the desire. She jumped when Mitchell touched her, pulled away if he tried to kiss her. His proximity was intolerable.

Veena works in supply chain. She has for years. She quit at twenty-nine when Neel was born, and then returned to the same job five years later, when he started kindergarten. Her company's software follows the life of a product, from its birth to its death. The orange: from the tree, to the truck, to Publix, to the brown bag. A bottle of shampoo: from the supplier, to warehouses, to salons around the country.

Her job is to make sure that the company's clients are happy, that the software is properly tracking their oranges and shampoo and books and purses and battery-operated puppies that somersault. If there are any problems, she is there to help.

At the client site today, the corporate offices of a major retail chain, she does what the in-house analysts should be able to do themselves. Inwardly rolling her eyes, she adjusts the system so that it sends a remote-control car to a warehouse in Tucson instead of Omaha. She doubles the shipments of a face cream to Kansas City and cuts in half what is being sent to Dayton, realizing by the end of the process that it is her company's software that is faulty, not the in-house analysts.

She finishes by noon and phones her office to say she is sick, unable to attend her afternoon meeting. Then she drives home and crawls into bed, choosing to skip lunch altogether, though her stomach is hollow with hunger. She skips lunch often. She will be thirty-eight in a month and her metabolism is waning.

When she wakes up from her nap she has a headache, and takes an ibuprofen. If she hurries, she might make it to the nature center before it closes. She pulls on a pair of jeans, a T-shirt, and her Tulane hoodie, and heads to the car.

At the exchange, Rosemary greets her.

"I've missed you. It's been months," she says. Her thick, long white hair is loose around her shoulders. Her blouse is covered with marsupials of all sorts, some that Veena recognizes, some that she does not, all with babies in their pouches.

"I just moved to the neighborhood," Veena says. "I'll be

coming more often." She says nothing about Mitchell or the separation. She takes the items out of the bag and sets them on Rosemary's desk. Veena looks up and checks, as she always does, for the antlers. There they are. Still gleaming.

"Don't worry, they're still available," Rosemary says. She looks down at what Veena has brought. The abalone shell, the mouse skull, the dead butterfly.

Rosemary does not ask questions about the objects. She enters points into Neel's account that Veena knows are too high. It is a silent transaction, a compassionate one, and one that breaks the rules. Only children are supposed to trade.

Veena does not thank Rosemary, though her gratitude is immense. She must leave as little room as possible for either of them to be implicated.

It was a school shooting. Neel was the only one who died. Two shots went into his body. One in his abdomen, one in his leg. Only one other person—the art teacher—was shot, but she escaped with minor injuries. An officer from the scene called them with the news. Neel was rushed to the hospital. Veena cannot remember the officer's name, only that he had lied. "He didn't tell us how bad it was," Veena later said to Mitchell. "He just said to come to the hospital."

"Would that have been the right thing to do?" Mitchell replied. "To tell us on the phone?"

Within ten minutes of the call, Veena and Mitchell were at Neel's side, his eyes closed, unconscious, his broken leg in a brace. He yawned a few times, his mouth in an O like an infant's, his lungs hungry for air. Then there was a terrible, soft gurgling sound. That was it.

His backpack had made it to the hospital somehow. In it was his lunchbox, and a brownie, half-eaten, that Veena had packed that morning. Before the staff wheeled him away, Veena sat and ate the rest of the brownie, turning the mushy bits in her mouth as she looked at Neel's shut eyes, the hair that would never be cut. She didn't offer any to Mitchell.

The man who killed Neel was forty-two years old, father to a five-year-old boy himself. Six months later, he was sentenced to life in prison. The night of the sentencing, neither Veena nor Mitchell could sleep. Mitchell because he thought it was not enough, Veena because she knew that nothing ever would be.

Days, weeks, and months go by. Spring turns to summer.

Veena's parents go to India, to visit her sick grandmother in Coimbatore.

"Can you take care of the plants while we're away?" her mother asks.

"I don't know," Veena says. It is an honest answer.

"Veena," her mother says. "Ammamma is dying, and the plants need water."

"Okay," Veena says.

"Veena?"

"Yes?"

"Please take care of yourself while we are gone."

Fall approaches. Veena runs, collects objects, goes to the nature center, eats takeout and prepared items she buys at Whole Foods. Her hip pain is persistent, but she gets used to it. Rosemary gets her up to 7,438 points.

Veena begins to order objects online to take into the nature center. Shells, coyote claws, and, for $24.99, a racoon skull. One day, unable to control the impulse, she orders three mid-sized geodes from Arizona for $150.

Every other Sunday, she goes to her childhood home to water her mother's plants, pinching off dead leaves, as her mother instructed her to. "The way to promote new growth is to get rid of the old," her mother said.

Her mother had wanted Neel to be cremated, as per Hindu tradition, but Veena and Mitchell buried him in Mitchell's family cemetery in Dallas.

"We only bury children who still have their milk teeth," her mother said. "Children of Neel's age should be cremated. We do not preserve the body, Veena. He will not be able to rest peacefully."

That was what she and her mother had fought about, that

two years later they still had not fully recovered from. *Baby teeth*. What would Neel say about baby teeth? *Living*.

One day in late September, Veena goes to the nature exchange and finds a college student behind the desk instead of Rosemary. The girl is toying with a scallop shell, carelessly bending it at its edge as she chews her gum.

"So your son isn't here? Is he sick?" the girl asks. Her jaw moves vigorously as she chews.

"Yes," Veena says.

"What happened?"

"Broken leg."

"He's sick and he broke his foot? Poor kid."

Veena nods. She takes out the objects she has brought: a flat, polished rock; an unusually large pine cone, and three inches of snake skin.

The girl writes a number down on a piece of paper and hands it to Veena.

"I'll enter it later," she says. "Computer's down, but give me your son's name."

"That's it?" Veena says. "Twenty-five points for all this?"

The girl blows a bubble and pops it with her tongue.

"This is how we do it," she says. "I went by the books."

Veena writes Neel's name down on the piece of paper and slides it towards the girl.

"Here's the account holder's name."

"You mean your son?" the girl says. "So you wanna pick something out? Poor kid might want something."

"He wants the antlers."

"Ten thousand points."

"I know. We're saving up."

"That's nice. He'll have to come in and get them himself though. That's the rule when it's a big prize like that," the girl says, an air of authority about her.

"He might not be better for months," Veena says.

"It might take months to get the points anyway."

"I don't know if he can come in."

"I mean, we can hold it for him if y'all decide on it," the girl says, her eyebrows furrowed.

"He's dead," Veena says. "He's been dead for two years."

The girl stops chewing her gum.

"But he did break his leg," Veena says, wishing she had left it at this in the first place. "He died with a broken leg."

The girl goes to a bin full of shells, sticks her hand in and fills Veena's paper bag.

"Take them," she says. "I won't tell my manager."

If Neel were alive, he would be nine, almost ten. Maybe reading *Harry Potter*, or having sleepovers. He would be moving towards adolescence, but he would still be sweet.

Still collecting his treasures and playing Lego with his best friend, Toby.

In the initial months after Neel's death, Veena tried many things. She took up yoga. She let an artist paint grief on her naked body. The artist had lost a child too, years ago. The artist wore loose, flowing skirts, and big hoop earrings. Her coppery hair was long and wild.

"I don't understand those mothers who don't want their babies to get bigger. The ones who want to freeze them in time," the artist said, as she painted a green line from Veena's belly button down to the top of her pelvis, just above the mound of hair.

"You hardly have scars," she said to Veena.

"I used stretch mark cream every day," Veena said. "I wish I hadn't."

Afterwards, Veena looked at herself in the full-length mirror mounted to the wall. It was a cheap mirror, and it made her look thinner than she was. She studied the art and ran her fingers over the dry paint. It would be photographed for her memory and then washed away in the shower the following day. Grief was an elongated lavender foxglove, its small bulbs alive but drooping. It was a cluster of rocks. Igneous, Neel would say. Red tulips. A small fountain of water. There were two brown lines on the rocks. Two squirrels in abstraction, maybe? And three streaks in the air. Butterflies?

"Why so many flowers?" Veena asked.

"Grief is alive," the artist said. "It's everywhere." Her eyes were anxious. "You don't like it?"

"It's beautiful," Veena said. "I wish I could see the beauty without the pain. Just for a moment."

When she showed Mitchell the art that evening, he looked away from her naked body, as if she were blinding him.

"Do what you need to do," he said.

"Isn't this hard for you?" she asked.

When he looked back at her his eyes were full and glistening. "You're making it harder."

Neither of them had any interest in activism, in fighting publicly against gun violence or school shootings. Time did nothing to change this. People called now and then: a father from Sandy Hook, a brother from Red Lake, a mother from Columbine, inviting them to join the cause, to campaign.

Instead, they sent generous checks. "This is all we can do right now," Mitchell said, speaking for both of them.

Six months after Neel died, right after the sentencing, Veena had a bench installed at his elementary school, with an ocean scene painted on it, a beach, waves, birds above. They shared a love for nature, mother and son. She had once worked at the aquarium, right after college.

Neel's class was there for the unveiling. There were still twenty-three children in the class, Neel's spot replaced by a brown-haired girl who moved from Michigan just weeks after the shooting.

The children planted an oak sapling next to the bench. Neel's teacher, Ms. Hackbarth, started the digging, and each child in the class took a turn. Two children placed the sapling in the ground and all the children took turns patting dirt around it, their small hands frantic and eager. Mitchell was out of town for a business trip. Veena had offered to reschedule the event.

"I'll see it soon enough," he promised.

After the planting was done, Ms. Hackbarth gave Veena a hug and sent each child in the class up to Veena to do the same. When Toby hugged her, Veena held him extra-long, sniffing him for any essence of her son that he might have retained. Then, single file, the children and their teacher went back into the school. Veena stayed in the playground alone, sitting on the bench.

Once a month, she still goes to the school and sits on the bench. She invited the artist who painted her body to join, but she never came. Mitchell came once or twice, but not after that.

"There are people who let their wounds heal and there are those who pick at them and pick at them," he said. "I can't be picking."

This month, she spends some time cleaning the bench, using wet wipes on the legs and on the seat. Then she sits and waits. Nobody comes.

•

The gum-chewing girl is there the next time Veena goes to the nature center, in early October.

"Hey," the girl says.

"I've got some good stuff," Veena says enthusiastically.

She opens her brown paper bag and takes out the three geodes she ordered from Arizona.

"Look, I'm really sorry about this," the girl says. "But your son's account has been deactivated."

"What do you mean?"

"The points belonged to him. Since he's gone, the account had to be deactivated."

Veena can't tell whether the girl is lying. She hears the words as if she, Veena, is reading them to herself, as if they were typed out and handed to her.

"Where's Rosemary?"

The girl sighs. She is not chewing gum today. "I feel really bad about this, but I don't make the rules."

"Where's Rosemary?"

"She's on vacation, visiting her grandchildren. This has nothing to do with her."

This girl was too young to understand. Veena had renewed her nature center membership on the phone for two years, keeping it at the family level, never taking Neel off.

"If you have other children, I could transfer the points," the girl offers.

"I don't have other children," Veena says.

•

At home, Veena feels sick. She takes a box of day-old cucumber sushi out of the fridge. She eats with her fingers, lifting each piece to her mouth, eating it dry, letting the rice and sesame scrape against her tongue, not bothering to open the soy sauce packet. It's a sign, she tells herself. She must not go back. Mitchell was right. She had to move on.

But the next day, she skips work and drives to the nature center. She bypasses the exchange and walks into the presentation hall, where she sits in the front row. A few families are there with young children, though the room is mostly empty. She has seen this same turtle presentation many times, with Neel.

The captive turtle's name is Felix. A woman named Barbara with a polo shirt and khakis and a white plastic name tag pinned to her chest takes Felix out of a deep wooden crate. The turtle inches forward.

Barbara explains that Felix has a friend, another captive turtle, named Felicia. They've been together for ten years.

A kid around nine or so raises a hand. "Do they have babies?" he asks.

Barbara shakes her head. "Good question." She reaches forward to pull Felix back. He's getting away.

"Even though we take care of them really well, in captivity they are under stress," Barbara says. Veena feels like

Barbara is looking at her. "It is very hard to reproduce under stress."

The kid's hand shoots up into the air again.

"Are they happy?" he asks.

"Well," Barbara says, "They are comfortable."

After Neel's death, Veena and Mitchell became like other childless adults who had no reason to be home early in the evenings, whose post-work hours were leisurely, a time to relax and read a book, to go for a quick run, or to even sneak in a short nap. Mitchell found some peace in all this, Veena did not.

Some times of the year were harder than others. Neither she nor Mitchell grew up celebrating Christmas—he was Jewish—and they never made a fuss over Santa or presents. It was actually Halloween, not Christmas, that was difficult for Veena now. What a cruel holiday it was, to make light of death and caskets, of bloody wounds, to bring packs of eager children to her doorstep.

Perhaps that is why, this year, Mitchell calls her on Halloween morning. It is the first call from him since she moved into the new house. She invites him to come over in the evening. When he says yes, she is surprised.

They drink cream soda mixed with Kahlúa in tall glasses

and sit on the living room couch waiting for kids to come. It is cool and breezy, the windows are open, the air brittle and fragrant with burning hickory from a neighbor's fire, a perfect night for trick-or-treating. At first, no one knocks, and Veena is anxious, but then dozens come, little ones with their parents, older ones in groups of five or six. Goldilocks. Annie. A decapitated ant holding its own head. A gaggle of geese. A pencil. Storm troopers.

When Veena runs out of candy and the doorbell rings again, she panics. Then she tells Mitchell to open the door and keep the kids waiting. She goes upstairs and comes back with Neel's tote.

At the door, she opens the tote for the costumed children: a spooky potato growing sprouts, a zombie rockstar, Harry Potter with a scar on the wrong side. They reach into the bag and retrieve a rock, a shell, a pine cone. "Cool!" the potato says. "Accio!" Harry Potter says.

After 8 p.m., the younger children stop coming and high schoolers show up. The big kids have put little effort into their costumes: a hobo, a girl in yellow sweats holding a sign that says "banana," a boy wearing a T-shirt that says "Too Cool for a Costume."

"They're too old to be here," Veena whispers to Mitchell, who is standing behind her with his glass. "I don't have anything for you," she says to them. She tries to shut the door, but Mitchell stops her, and presents Neel's tote to them.

"Take something," he orders.

The teenagers reach in and pull objects out, a piece of sea glass, an arrowhead, a lotus seed pod, dry and hard, the color of rust.

The banana girl throws the pod to the ground and crushes it with the tip of her yellow sneakers.

"Let's go," she says. "There's nothing for us here."

One of the boys throws the arrowhead into the bushes.

"Weirdos," the other one says.

"Give them back if you don't want them," Veena shouts as they walk away.

A rock comes flying towards her and hits the side of her bad hip.

"Hey!" she shouts, but the kids run off, and Mitchell leads her inside, to the couch.

She does not protest.

He pulls back the edge of her jeans and inspects her. There's a small red bruise. He touches it and she winces.

Her head on his chest, she tells him about the canceled nature exchange account. How she feels like she cannot go on without the antlers. There is nothing she wants more. She sobs.

"I'll get you antlers," he says. He kisses her, first on each of her eyes, and then on her lips. Now he is crying too. "I'll buy some. I'll order some."

"I want *those* antlers," she says. "Neel's antlers."

"Okay, I'll get them for you," he says.

They are careless, his words, but they give her hope.

She licks the salt of her own tears and then, her voice a heavy hush, says, "Come upstairs."

She goes to the nature center one final time, with Mitchell. It is a Sunday. The plan is his: walk in, make a large donation, ask for the antlers.

"Whatever they want," he says, "I'll give it to them."

A sense of adventure fills her as they drive, a sense of pursuit. But when they get to the center, there are no antlers, just the gum-chewing girl at the desk whose name Veena still cannot remember. Since they last met, the girl has pierced her earlobes, Veena notices.

"Someone claimed them," the girl says. "Just this week."

"You have them in the back!" Veena says accusingly. "I know you do."

"No," the girl says.

Veena strides past the girl's desk, opening a door that says "Staff Only," shouting, "I'll find them. You're keeping them away from me."

How could she come so close and have it end like this? She feels that she is two Veenas now, one version of her unable to control the other.

"Hey, what are you doing?" the girl says. "Hey." She looks at Mitchell. "You need to stop her."

"Veena, honey," Mitchell says, following her in.

"Help me," Veena says. "Or stay away."

The girl is on her phone, calling for help.

The backroom is full of shelves, like a warehouse. Veena walks up and down the four aisles, opening the largest of the plastic bins she can reach in search of the antlers. She moves quickly. Mitchell catches up. He puts his arms around her, his grasp tight. She fights it.

"Stop, Veena. Stop."

"I need to find them."

The girl is in the back room now too. And Rosemary is there. Veena stops trying to escape Mitchell's grasp, and studies Rosemary's blouse. It is covered with acorns. Neel hated acorns. He hated them because they were so plentiful, so easy to find. So boring.

Veena wriggles out of Mitchell's arms and starts opening bins again, throwing things to the ground in fury, surprised by her own recklessness.

"Tell me where they are," she shouts at the girl, who has stopped chewing her gum. "Tell me!"

Rosemary walks up to Veena, coming closer until they

are nose to nose. Veena has never been this close to her, close enough to smell her. Lavender perfume, and under that, a trace of staleness, something musty. Raspberry-colored lipstick, breath like oranges. And one long white hair sprouting from her chin. *Living*, Veena can't help but think.

"The antlers exist," Rosemary says. "Just because they aren't here anymore, it doesn't mean they don't exist."

Veena cannot stand any longer. She collapses to the floor, draws her knees to her chest, and rocks back and forth. The rocks, the shells, the pine cones, the antlers, everything belonged to those who were alive. That's what Rosemary was saying, wasn't it?

She feels light-headed, a little dizzy. She looks up and knows how it seems to them. Their faces, all their faces, are twisted with pity. The older woman understands her pain, the younger one is alarmed. Mitchell is alive and present, but too long in her company and he would decay.

For now, she has no choice but to stay where she is. In order to exist, she cannot choose life, just as she did not choose death.

"Why?" Veena says. "Why does someone else get to have them?"

If one of them answers her, she does not hear it. Instead, it is her own voice that speaks to her. In her hands, the antlers had no future. They belonged in the home of the boy from the park, or Toby's, in the hands of the active, curious, living child who had carefully collected points, and proudly claimed it for his bookshelf.

Mitchell offers her his hand. "Come," he says, his voice gentle, and patient. They walk to the parking lot hand in hand. She knows that when they get home, he will not come inside.

His Holiness

The old white man first showed up two months ago. He sits on a metal folding chair in the temple lobby, at the bottom of the stairs that lead to the sanctum. He is always off to the side, in nobody's way. In his hands, he holds wooden beads the color of milk chocolate, strung together with white thread. He chants all day long, until closing time. *Sri Ram, Jai Ram, Jai Jai Ram.* "He pauses only to use the bathroom," Neela's mother tells her. "He chants softly, but some are saying it is a nuisance."

Her mother is hunched over the kitchen counter, making a neat pile of Neela's SAT registration forms, and the directions to the testing site.

"How does it matter, if he isn't bothering anyone?" Neela asks.

"It doesn't bother me," her mother says. "Others say he should go to the Hare Krishna temple, you know, where the white people go. If you came to the temple one day, you could see him for yourself. I wanted you to go before the SATs anyway, to get blessings for your test."

Neela sees her mother squint at the clock on the wall above the couch, next to the framed family portrait of Neela and her parents. "We can still make it tonight, before it closes," her mother says.

Neela rolls her eyes. "I need my sleep before the test. See you in the morning."

It was her second time taking the exam. The first time her parents had done everything. They prayed at home every day, and then did a special puja at the temple that cost $301 and required her mother to fry 108 vadas made of gram flour and black pepper.

Her score was not even good enough for Penn State. Neela wants, at the very least, to get into Penn State. She would like to study international affairs, maybe join the foreign service and travel the world. That is her current dream anyway. Her father says it is fine. Her mother urges her to consider something that offers more stability—teaching school even, or physical therapy. "Best to travel for vacation, not work," her mother says.

The morning of the exam, Neela's mother pulls the car up to the entrance of the testing site, a public high school one town over.

"Okay, do well, kanna," her mother says, as she hands Neela a brown paper bag full of granola bars and packets of trail mix. "That Colin is picking you up? I will be at the hospital when you're done."

"Yes, Amma," Neela says. She steps out and slings her backpack over one shoulder.

"Just do your best," her mother says as Neela shuts the door.

When she finishes the test—exhausted and unsure of whether her best will be good enough—it's nearly noon, and Colin is waiting for her. They drive to Monroeville Mall and smoke cigarettes in the parking lot, as they do once a week. They throw the butts on the ground and stomp on them, as if they are killing an animal under their feet. Then they go inside and walk back and forth along the mall's two levels, hoping to spot Tom Hanks Not the Actor, who is both Colin's secret crush and the school's star lacrosse player.

When Colin drops her off, Neela gives him a peck on the cheek and tells him to cheer up. "Don't waste too much time thinking about him," she says. "You're better than that."

It is the last day of summer vacation, and tomorrow is the first day of Neela's senior year. Soon the homework will pile up, and she will be busy with college applications, essays, and drama club. She and Colin are set designers for drama club, a role that Neela's mother thinks takes too much time without offering much in return.

"Nobody will ever recognize you for doing background work," her mother says.

As soon as the school year begins, she and her mother will resume their fights about these things, but today she is free, the rest of the day hers to enjoy.

On the kitchen counter, she finds a plate of steamed idlis covered with Saran wrap. In a small Pyrex with a blue lid, there is mint chutney. Neela takes the lid off and her mouth begins to water from the fragrance of the blended mint. After Neela's father started going on tour, her mother took extra nursing shifts to make more money, but somehow she still found time to cook.

There is a yellow Post-it stuck to the counter in between the plate of idlis and the bowl of chutney. Neela reads her mother's scrawl.

"Appa called from Sedona. Here is his hotel number. Call him back."

Neela sprinkles water on the idlis so they stay soft and fluffy, then shoves the plate into the microwave. She eats standing at the kitchen counter, breaking pieces off with her fingers, dunking the pillowy chunks into the tangy chutney, licking the bits that stick to her fingers.

While she eats, she looks at the family portrait hanging in the living room, above the sagging brown love seat. The photo was taken at Olan Mills when she was twelve, when her unplucked eyebrows met in a V. In it, her mother is wearing a sari the color of cantaloupe flesh, her father a blue pinstriped shirt. Neela is wearing a red velvet dress. She studies her father's image in the picture. This is the father she once knew, the one who drove her to soccer games, sat up front during school programs to get good video footage, who clumsily braided her hair when her mother was away visiting family in India.

Neela goes upstairs, peels off her jeans and top, and puts on running shorts and a white sports bra. She pulls her long black hair, a streak of it dyed bright blue, into a thick ponytail. Then she slips a Verve CD into her Discman, clips it to her waistband, and leaves the house running.

When she gets back, she collapses onto her parents' bed, sweaty, props herself against the pillows that line the headboard, and drinks a can of Mountain Dew while watching reruns of *Friends*, *The Cosby Show*, and *Hangin' with Mr. Cooper*. None of the shows make her laugh, but she sinks deeper into the bed, body slouched, and watches anyway, delighting in her laziness, kicking her socks off halfway through the first episode.

At eight in the evening, the phone rings. The caller ID says Arizona. She ignores the call. Then she gets into the shower, to avoid a lecture from her mother.

When her mother gets back from the hospital, she tells Neela that she will be going to the temple the following day.

"For the night puja," she says. "Will you come with me?"

Neela shrugs and her mother says, "You won't have homework on the first day of school. Did you ever call Appa?"

"I'll come with you to the temple," Neela says. Her hair, still wet from the shower, drips onto the kitchen floor.

To some degree every Indian in Pittsburgh, Neela included, is proud of the temple. It was the first Hindu temple of its size in North America, built in the late 1970s by Indians who came to Pittsburgh to work at Westinghouse and Alcoa, to practice medicine at Pitt, to study or teach at Carnegie Mellon. Since Pittsburgh sits at the junction of three rivers—the Ohio, the Allegheny, and the Monongahela—Indians all over the country thought it a most auspicious location. Early donations for the temple came from as far as Anchorage, Alaska, and Seattle, Washington. The temple's carved white spires, chiseled by artisans brought in from Madurai, were featured in *Architectural Digest.*

Neela's parents were part of a later, larger crop of Indians who came in the '80s and were eternally grateful for the work of their predecessors. Neela went to the temple often with her parents when she was young, to play with her friends, eat the cafeteria food, and watch the fireworks on Diwali that the temple had special permission to launch.

For Neela's parents, it was a place to pray, but also a place to gather, to be part of something bigger than their small family unit.

Today when she enters the temple with her mother, Neela immediately sees the old white man. Her mother ignores him, but Neela cannot help but stare.

He is smiling, and he looks peaceful, not strange or scary. He is just an ordinary old white man, the kind you might see standing in the checkout line at Giant Eagle, or buying screws at the hardware store. The grandfatherly type, with skin that looks worn and soft. He is wearing a brown wool beret.

"Cap is new," Neela's mother whispers once they pass him. "He started wearing it a few weeks ago."

In the sanctum, Indu Aunty is singing a lullaby. The priest is rocking the goddess Lakshmi to sleep in a cradle. One by one, he will rock each god to sleep as Aunty sings. Neela thinks she could fall asleep here too, surrounded by the idols. She always resists coming to the temple with her mother, but once she arrives, she finds that the burning incense and camphor calm her, that the ring of the priest's bell and the temple's black stone walls are deeply comforting.

Each God in the temple has a duty, to create life or destroy it, to shower wealth, to provide knowledge, to thwart evil. The elephant-headed Ganesha removes obstacles. Neela imagines herself next to him, curled into a cozy ball.

After the priest puts every god to sleep with a short prayer, he comes around with balls of sweetened semolina and fruit.

"How are you?" he asks Neela. He speaks in Tamil. "Long time you have not come."

Neela forces herself to smile at him.

"I was busy," she replies in English.

The priest gives two apples to Neela's mother.

"One for him," he says.

Neela's mother nods. "Thank you," she says. "He will be home in a few days."

"Come back soon," the priest says to Neela. "In the temple, we can all find peace."

After the puja, Neela and her mother go to the temple cafeteria to eat tamarind rice and sambar rice. The food is available daily for a one-dollar donation, and packed in small, square foam boxes. The lemon pickle is free. On Sundays, there are ladoos.

"Welcome, welcome," the chef behind the counter says. His name is Ram, and he is from Rameshwaram; a short, plump man who knows every regular and not-so-regular cafeteria patron.

"Glad you brought her," he says, nodding towards Neela.

They choose a table in the cafeteria and sit to eat; no one else is there. Then Neela's mother heads outside to the car while Neela stops to use the restroom. It is closing time at the temple, and the lights throughout the building are slowly being shut off. Neela walks by the old man, still sitting in the metal chair, still chanting. She shivers, and hugs herself. When she hears footsteps coming from behind, she walks faster. The footsteps only grow louder, so she moves quickly towards the exit, but not fast enough. Just before she reaches the temple's main door, she feels a palm on her shoulder. She turns to see that the hand on her shoulder is also holding a string of prayer beads, and they dangle by her side. The old white man's other hand is in a fist. Neela cannot breathe. She wonders whether her mother will come back in to look for her, or whether the priest upstairs will hear her if she screams.

"You dropped something," the man says. Up close, Neela can see the fine wrinkles on his face, like cuts that have healed. She sees, too, that his cheekbones are gaunt, that his skin is loose. He opens his fist, and shows her an earring shaped like a maple leaf. Neela takes it from him.

"Thank you," she says. "I did not know it fell off."

"Have a good night," he says. "It's almost time for me to go home, too."

In the morning, Neela gathers her books for school. She stuffs them into her backpack and zips it closed. Her father is due back tomorrow, her mother has told her, on a flight that will arrive early in the morning. She spots a red flyer sticking out from a stack of papers on her desk. It says, "Spiritual Leader and Scholar-Mystic returns to Pittsburgh for Special Seminar." She pulls it out, looks it over, and then discards it.

During study hall, her last period of the day, Neela reads her biology book. The first quiz of the year is on amino acids. She yawns. Colin, sitting behind her, pokes her back with a pencil. Neela shuts her textbook and turns around.

"Hey," he says. "Tom Hanks Not the Actor touched me today."

His grin is wide, his eyes teasing. Neela is stumped by Colin's infatuation, how it takes up so much of his time, how it both torments him and gives him delight.

"Does he even know who you are?" Neela says. "Tom Hanks isn't even cute. He's old."

"I was walking down the hall and our arms, like, totally touched."

"He likes girls."

"That's what he thinks."

"Shut up," Neela says. She laughs too loudly, and Mr. Bryer calls out their names.

"Miss Prasad, Mr. Tupper. Study Hall is a silent period."

Neela opens her biology book again. This time, it falls to a chapter at the back of the book, one the teacher will never get to. There is a picture of a rooster on this page. Neela reads about a strange phenomenon observed in chicken coops. When no aggressive male is present, a hen will step forward, the book says. The hen transitions, and grows fierce talons and wattles under her chin. Eventually, a red cockscomb emerges from the top of her head. The other hens might ignore her at first, but when she crows, they accept her. The transformation is complete. She is a rooster. "Spontaneous sex reversal," the book says.

When Neela gets home from school, she notices that the old family picture in the living room is gone. In its place, there is a framed portrait of her father—the new version of her father. His hair is long; his beard unkempt. He is wearing his saffron-colored robes.

Neela walks into the kitchen, where her mother is boiling a large pot of tomato rasam, twisting black pepper into the soupy concoction with a grinder. Even from a few feet away, the pepper tickles Neela's nose.

"I found cigarettes in your jeans again," her mother says, without turning around. "How will you ever get anywhere? Wasting your time with that Colin. If your father were here . . ."

"He isn't," Neela says.

"Neela."

"Where did you put the picture from the living room?" Neela asks. "The one of all of us?"

"It's still there. Moved to the corner, by the fern. I thought Appa might like to see this one when he comes back."

"You thought he might like it better than our family picture? Because he only cares about himself!" She is nearly shouting.

Her mother sighs as she stirs the rasam.

"Your father cares about us, Neela. I know this is hard for you to understand right now."

"Do you even feel married to him anymore?"

Neela's mother puts the wooden spoon down, turns around, and slaps Neela across the face.

"Amma!" Neela backs away.

"Sorry, Neela. I'm so sorry."

Her mother wipes her hand on her shirt, as if it is wet. She turns off the stove. In her wrinkled hospital scrubs, she looks completely spent.

"I think I need to lie down for a moment, Neela. Eat if you're hungry, will you? Rice is in the cooker."

Neela's father arrives the next morning while she is still sleeping. Lying in bed, she listens to her parents downstairs, and hears her mother's girlish giggle in response to whatever her father said. He is home for only a few days, as always. Soon he will leave to do a workshop at some sort of hippie farm outside Boston.

By the time Neela emerges, her mother has left for work.

"Hi, Appa."

She does not stop to hug him, reaching instead for the box of cinnamon squares that sits on top of the refrigerator.

"How was your flight?"

"Good. How are your classes?"

"Fine."

"How are your teachers this year?"

"Okay."

"Theater starting?"

"Soon. Colin and I are head of set."

"Shall I drop you to school?"

"I'm fine walking."

After she eats, she grabs a banana from the counter and leaves in a hurry, not wishing to stay and pack herself a lunch.

In the evening, Neela and her parents go to a Burmese restaurant they all like. Her father is not wearing his saffron-colored robes. He is wearing the clothes Neela once associated with him: a button-down shirt, slacks, and Velcro sneakers.

"Velcro is the most amazing of inventions," he was fond of saying, when Neela was little.

When they arrive at Rangoon House, they bump into Neela's old friend Maisie, who is there with her parents.

Maisie and Neela are no longer close because Maisie has become popular, a tennis player and cheerleader who hangs out with Tom Hanks Not the Actor. In middle school Maisie and Neela liked to knit scarves together, and make friendship bracelets. They had sleepovers and practiced putting on their mothers' makeup. They have grown apart, but they share a familial intimacy when they pass each other in the hallway at school—a nod, a smile, a respectful acknowledgment of a time that has passed.

"Oh, hi, Neela!" Maisie says. "Haven't seen you at school yet this year. No classes together. Bummer."

Maisie's gaze shifts to Neela's father. She looks at his long, scraggly beard and his knotty hair. Despite the familiar clothes he wears tonight, there is little sign of the college lecturer Maisie knew from their younger days.

"Nice to see you, Mr. Prasad, Mrs. Prasad," Maisie says politely, though Neela can hear her voice wavering. Then Maisie looks at Neela and drops her volume to a whisper.

"Wow."

"God bless you, Maisie," Neela's father says when Maisie says bye.

Over her bowl of Burmese curry, Neela says she will not attend her father's event at the community center in the city.

"But we must support your father," her mother says. "He came here to do this."

"Not to see us?"

"Prabha, we should not force her," her father says. He turns to Neela. "Of course I am here to see you."

He puts his arm around Neela's shoulder, but she pulls away.

The next day is Saturday, so Neela goes for a long morning run. She runs hard, up and down the hills of her neighborhood, her calves burning, her lips salty with sweat. She stops when she reaches Ferri's, the grocery store where Colin works.

"It's on the house," Colin says, when she tries to pay for her smoothie. "I'm allowed one a day, and I clearly don't need it." He pats his belly.

"Anything new with Tom Hanks Not the Actor?"

"No," Colin says, pouting. "I heard that he might ask Alice Chang to Homecoming." He sighs dramatically. "What I would give to be Alice Chang."

When Neela gets home from her run, her father is gone.

"I should be there already, helping to set up," her mother says, "but I said I would bring you."

"No! I told you. No."

She walks upstairs and slams the door to the bathroom. After her shower she hears a honk, and peers out her bedroom window to see her mother sitting in their gray sedan in the driveway, looking up at her.

Neela knows she could wait it out—her mother will leave eventually, so as not to miss the session. But she decides to get dressed and go after all; not for her father, but for her mother. Neela suspects her mother is hurting just as much as she is, though the rules of adulthood don't allow her to show it.

Neela pulls the hood of her gray sweatshirt over her head, and huffs as she clicks her seat belt into place. Her mother is wearing dressy slacks, a silky light blue shirt, and white pearls. She looks pretty, and young, with makeup on. Her hair is half up, the way she fixes it when she is going out somewhere special.

"You look nice," Neela says.

"Thank you."

During the thirty-minute drive, Neela's mother plays Lord Krishna bhajans, and Neela finds herself involuntarily rocking back and forth gently as the singer calls out an alternate name for Krishna. "Govinda, Govinda, Govinda," he sings, his voice a little louder and more ecstatic each time he says the word.

"He makes even less money than he used to," Neela says, when there is a break in the singing.

"It is not about the money, Neela. I want him to be happy."

The event is in a dingy community center. Neela's mother sits in the front, but Neela sits in the very last row. The room is windowless; the walls are bare and the lights are fluorescent. There are about thirty people in the audience, all sitting on folding chairs. Almost all of the attendees are white, Neela notes. Two are black. One is Asian. In front of Neela, there is a scruffy-faced man with three bags at his side, two plastic and one cloth duffel. He smells like the train station near her grandparents' home in India.

"Suffering is a choice," Neela's father begins. "We alone have the power to relieve ourselves from it."

Neela slumps into her chair. Her father's words exhaust her. He looks so confident as he speaks to the audience. At one point, he makes eye contact with Neela. His eyes linger for a second too long and Neela looks at the floor, unwilling to grant him the connection.

When she can't take it anymore, she leaves the room. She will not watch while people line up to meet her father after his talk. She knows exactly what he does, how he places his hand over their heads to give his blessings. In the corridor, she sees a donation box stuffed with a few five- and ten-dollar bills. The middle-aged blond woman minding the box smiles at Neela and, not knowing who she is, offers her a book: her father's self-published self-help guide to peace and happiness.

"They are free. A ten-dollar donation if you would like. Are you a student at Pitt?"

"No." Neela eyes the woman suspiciously. "I have a copy of it at home."

The woman nods and then busies herself by arranging the stack of books.

"What made you like him?" Neela asks while she fishes through her purse. The woman looks back up at Neela.

"You're way too young to understand this. But when you're in a bad place, a really bad place, and someone tells you things will get better, that he *believes* in you—it changes everything."

The woman stops talking.

"Glad he helped you." Neela takes a cigarette out of her purse and sees the woman's alarmed expression. "Don't worry, I'll take it outside."

After she smokes, she throws the cigarette on the ground and stomps on it. Back inside, her mother says she has been looking for her.

"We need to help clean up. And you smell terrible. When will you stop spending time with that Colin?"

They put the folding chairs away and sweep the room while her father puts his books and the donation box in the car.

When her father first started holding sessions, when Neela was just starting high school, nobody came. Then a few people started attending, and he was exuberant. "This is how it starts," he would say during their family dinners. At the end of Neela's freshman year, he quit his job as a college lecturer, declaring that he could not be a poor scholar of religion any longer. A permanent teaching position was never going to come along; it was hopeless to think it would. Industry was out of the question—who wanted a religious scholar? They were surrounded by engineers and scientists and doctors, aunties and uncles from the temple who did not know that Neela, for a brief time, had qualified for reduced-price school lunches, that her mother had bought only the quick-sale vegetables at Giant Eagle. Still, they were doing okay. They were not poor. Neela remembers her mother pleading with her father to keep his job.

"Between my job at the hospital, and your work at the university, we make it work. We have enough."

"I need a change."

"But this is what you want to do?"

"This is what I must do," he said. Religion was the business he knew, the one he had studied from its very origins. To Neela, it felt like he was giving up, becoming someone he was not because the world demanded a certain kind of success.

When Neela was twelve—the same age she was in that framed family photo—her parents took her to Disney World. She had begged for the trip after seeing commercials on television. Her mother said it was too expensive. But on the first day of Thanksgiving Break, early in the morning, Neela's father took her to the driveway. She was still in her pajamas. He pointed to the car.

"Get in," he said, his eyes twinkling. He and her mother had packed it with their things the night before.

They drove to Florida on snowy roads, saving the money they would have spent on plane fare. In the parking lot of a Wendy's in Roanoke, West Virginia, they stopped to put chains on the tires. Her father had tried first, but could not tolerate the cold and the chains kept getting tangled up. It was Neela's mother who managed to lay them out and then wrap them around the tires. It was her mother, too, who drove the car forward so they could snap the chains in place.

When they reached Florida, her mother learned that if they went on a tour of a time-share property, they could get free tickets to the amusement parks.

"No hanky-panky?" Neela's father said to the woman who was doing the tour. "We just take the tour and get the tickets?"

"Yes," the woman had promised, her white teeth and shiny heels gleaming in the sun. The tour took a whole day. There were walkthroughs of three condos, followed by a lunch of sandwiches on white bread at the golf course and long sales pitches. By the end of it, Neela was ready to return to the hotel and sleep. Her father complained that they should have bought the tickets outright.

“They stole our time.”

“But we saved money,” her mother said. “We couldn’t afford this trip in the first place.”

Neela loved the Magic Kingdom. For two days, she ran from ride to ride. When Princess Jasmine appeared, Neela posed with her, an awestruck child again.

One evening, Neela and her parents went to a diner that smelled like dirty school cafeteria dishes, located halfway between the Magic Kingdom and their hotel. Neela spotted Captain Hook there, putting a spoon of ice cream into Princess Jasmine’s mouth. Neither was in costume, but Hook’s mustache was real, and Neela recognized it.

Her father smirked when she pointed them out. “You know those people are actors with real lives, don’t you?”

“Of course,” Neela said, though she had been mesmerized all day, convinced that the unreal was real, that magic was possible.

“Don’t you know Mickey Mouse is a woman?” her mother added, teasing.

Her father threw his head back and laughed; her mother’s eyes were lit. Neela wasn’t hurt by the joking, though it was at her expense, because she loved to see her mother this way, loved how wide her smile was, how pleased her mother was to make her father laugh.

•

In the car ride home after her father's lecture, Neela sits in the back. She pulls her hoodie up over her head and leans against the door. Her father is talking to her mother, and it is all about his business. He is thrilled about the evening's turnout, the six books he sold. Neela feels something knot up in her stomach. Her father is playing dress-up like the actor who played Captain Hook. It was humiliating, that he had to resort to this.

The next morning, Neela finds her father sitting cross-legged on the couch. As she eats her cinnamon squares he reads the Sunday *Post-Gazette* in his hands. His own portrait hangs above him. Her mother is at work already.

"One day, they might cover my events."

He puts the paper down on the sofa.

"What do you think?"

"Maybe."

"Come. I know this is hard for you. Sit with me."

He is wearing a plain white kurta pajama and his hair is tied into a bun. Neela leaves the cinnamon squares in the kitchen, and sits cross-legged on the patterned Persian carpet in front of her father, facing him as if she is one of his followers.

"Pretty earrings."

"You bought them for me. Maple leaves from Quebec."

"That reminds me," he says. He goes to the kitchen and

comes back with a small paper bag. "I bought this for you in Sedona."

Neela opens it and pulls out a red rock, a smooth sphere.

"The rock formations there are stunning. The gods live among them. I am sure of it. You see them as the sun rises and sets, their faces smiling at you under the light. It's like . . ."

He stops, worried he has upset her.

"It's fine. Preach to me. You need the practice."

Neela knows how obstinate she sounds. How rude.

"I'd like to take you someday, that's all."

"You don't have to do this, you know. You could stay home. Or do what you used to do. I could get a job at Ferri's if we need extra money. Colin gets five-fifty an hour."

"Your mother makes enough money for the family, Neela. I have learned to accept that. What I am doing now is building a business. It will take time, but my heart is in this work."

"Work? This is work? This is a scam."

"It is good for me, and good for the people."

Neela looks at her father, dressed in his cotton pajamas. In the framed portrait above him, his right palm faces forward, an offer of blessing to anyone who looks his way. Neela wonders whether this version of her father hangs in the homes of any followers. If not, would it someday? She hopes not.

"You're a fake," she says.

Neela's father shakes his head. "As time goes by, maybe you will understand."

He stands up and reaches out to hug her, but she steps back. Her eyes are wet. Both her father and the framed portrait above him are blurry now. She blinks. That he was doing this for money was difficult to accept, but that he believes he is doing good is an insanity she cannot process.

"Neela," he says softly.

"I'm going for a run."

She races through the streets of her neighborhood in her sports bra and shorts, in spite of the cold. In a matter of days, summer has turned to fall. She runs down to Ferri's, up the hill to the high school, and back home again, cutting as fast as she can through the brisk air. She feels the weight of her body each time a foot touches the ground, but also a lightness, a sense that she can go anywhere, do anything. When she comes back home, her father has left for the airport, off to his next lecture. She collapses on the couch, closes her eyes, and feels as if she is floating in dark space, like she is both a single particle and many, minuscule but expansive; it is a feeling beyond her understanding.

Neela turns on the television, but instead of what is on the screen she sees her father: in his taxi, his suitcase full of books, his shoulder bag containing his notebook, a water bottle, and the snacks her mother packed for him. In his wallet, she knows, he keeps a picture of her. In the photo she is six years old, her hair in two tight braids, and she is standing in the lobby of the Carnegie Library in Pittsburgh. Her father is at her side. In the photo he is thirty, a graduate student on the brink of getting his doctorate. Neela knows that it was a stressful time for her father. He received no promising job offers, which led to his taking the position at the university as a part-time lecturer. It was never his dream.

Neela imagines her father boarding the plane, taking his seat, and pulling out the photograph, showing it to the passenger next to him proudly.

"My daughter."

Neela had loved going to the library with him back then. It was a grand place, with its domed ceiling and marble stairs that led up to a room of old library books for sale. In the lobby, Neela often knelt to run her fingers over the intricate tiles.

In the photo, above where Neela and her father are standing, there is a painting of Andrew Carnegie. The industrialist is dressed in a suit, standing as erect as a preacher, with a book tucked under his arm.

"They called him the robber baron," Neela remembers her father saying. "He made a lot of money and then gave it all away. See that book under his arm? *The Gospel of Wealth*."

Those words, “robber baron,” had stuck with Neela for years, their sound and meaning strange and indelible.

That evening, when she gets home from a long day at the hospital, Neela’s mother hands her a copy of the *Post-Gazette.* She points to an obituary. The old white man is wearing his beret in the picture. He was a retired schoolteacher from West Lafayette. Towards the end, he found a new kind of spirituality, the paper said. “He went to the S.V. Temple every day.” It was a cancer of the blood. Once it started spreading, he wanted nothing but to spend his last days at the temple. He had gone to India as a young man on a Fulbright scholarship, and ever since had been a devout Hindu.

“His family wants to hold a memorial service at the temple,” her mother says. “You should have heard the drama at the meeting last week, discussing the possibility. One half said *absolutely not*; the other half said *why not?*”

The chairman of the temple board had quieted the patrons by announcing that the family was donating thirty thousand dollars to the temple. The old man’s son was a successful engineer in Silicon Valley. It was enough money to start a renovation project, to bring craftsmen from India to Pittsburgh once again to carve new deities and build their abodes out of stone. “Can you believe it? That poor man. And such generosity from the family,” her mother said. “Of course, the chairman reminded us all that to give to God is to give to good."

Still in her blue scrubs, her smell a mixture of sweat and hospital disinfectant, Neela's mother sits down next to her daughter and puts her arm around her. Neela turns on the television. The two fall into silence as a raven-haired meteorologist on WTAE talks. It may snow a few inches next week, though it is still fall, and portions of the Ohio, the Allegheny, and the Monongahela could freeze over.

No. 16 Model House Road

Mornings in Bangalore are typically crisp and cool, but this morning there is a bit of warm sun and it streams through the grilled window, casting a shadow of bars that stretch underneath Latha and Muthu's round glass-topped coffee table. The developer woman has her papers spread out over the glass, one page right on top of the plate of butter biscuits that Latha set out: sketches, floor plans, and photographs detailing what things could be like.

"You could have three bedrooms, even four," the woman says. Right now, they have only two.

Latha's fingers tug at a loose strand of wicker on the arm of the love seat. She is sitting next to Muthu on the well-worn pale green cushions, observing the woman across from her with great curiosity. The woman's toenails are painted a shade of light blue that reminds Latha of the soap she uses when she does the laundry. She is wearing linen pants and a red cotton shirt, appropriately high-necked and pleasantly loose, with a stylish outward flare at the waist. One of her legs is crossed over the other, and the boldness of this shocks Latha. Not because she thinks women should not cross their legs. She believes that women can do anything. Her own daughter works, and she sees women working on the TV serials she watches. Latha is shocked because, for the first time, she is observing a woman at work—with the style, posture, and demeanor of a professional—right in front of her, in her home.

The woman directs her words towards Muthu, though it is Latha who actually owns No. 16 Model House Road. Binny left it to her when she died, not him.

"The living area will increase by fifty percent with most options," the woman says, her English clean and crisp. "Remarkable what we can do."

The developer's proposal is simple: to demolish Latha's beloved No. 16, and in its place erect a thoughtfully constructed, modern low-rise apartment building. Four stories. Four flats. All costs covered by the company. During the year it would take to construct the new building, the company would cover the cost of Latha and Muthu's housing with a generous lump sum. At the end of it all, the bottom flat would go to Latha and Muthu, and the other three would go to the developer and be sold at a big profit.

It was a scheme happening all over Bangalore in various forms as the city's tech industry grew at an explosive rate. Property values were higher than they had ever been, and housing was almost impossible to find. A few years ago, another developer had offered to buy their plot. Theirs was just a one-and-a-quarter-ground plot but that developer was willing to pay them three crores for it. They declined.

Today, the woman has four layouts for Latha and Muthu to choose from. Latha is partial to the smallest of the floor plans because it offers the most garden space. But she knows Muthu will disregard it.

While Muthu studies the plans, Latha continues to study the woman. Her hair is long, loose, and straight, cut unevenly in the front so that pieces of it touch her cheeks and chin. The unevenness appears to be intentional. She is in her early thirties, Latha thinks, based on her still-firm skin and the presence of a single visible gray hair that runs down from her side part. She is not wearing a thaali around her neck, or a ring, but that means nothing in Bangalore these days. Even Latha's daughter, newly married, only wears her thaali when attending a wedding or some other family function.

"From the beginning, I have liked this one," Muthu says. He points to a layout that appears to have an extra room jutting out the back.

From the beginning.

Muthu had wanted to take the deal after the first proposal, nearly ten months ago. The woman is the fourth person from the company to come to their home. Latha can't help but wonder if the choice to send a woman this time was intentional. Was it possible that they knew it was Latha, not Muthu, who was delaying the decision?

The woman smells good. Not flowery or spicy, but like damp earth, that complex smell that emanates when rain hits soil. Latha wonders whether she uses an imported perfume.

"Good choice," the woman says to Muthu. "The Bonus Room option. Our most spacious. It has the largest kitchen." Then, finally, she looks at Latha. "What do you think? You have not said a thing."

Under the woman's gaze, Latha becomes conscious of her own physical presence. Her hair smells like coconut oil. It is not cut to different lengths. It is pulled back into a bun, and there are no purposeless wisps on her face. Half of her hair has gone white. Her toenails are unpainted. She is aware that she looks like a meek housewife in her old, wrinkled cotton sari. But still—has this woman really finally turned to her, only to ask her about the *kitchen*? After they had been sitting there for so long.

"Will that room extend into the back garden?" Latha asks. It takes her a moment too long to get the words out.

"Yes," the woman says. Latha watches as the woman uncrosses her legs and recrosses them the other way. "But we understand the value of green space. There will be a small, shared garden. We can do a little planting for you, if you would like."

A shared garden. If you would like. The words are eerily

similar to what the doctor said all those years ago, when Latha was eleven weeks into her first pregnancy. "There is no heartbeat. There is a procedure we can do to expedite the matter, *if you would like*." That doctor had been old and sloppily dressed, nothing like this woman. But they were alike in their thoughtlessness. Latha rarely thinks about the miscarriage, with two healthy children now, both grown. But she remembers how helpless she felt at the doctor's words, and she feels the same now. Like there is nothing she can do to change her situation.

Latha points to the option with the smallest square footage and the biggest garden. The garden, shaped like a boxy L, is colored green on the paper. "What about this?"

"Too small," Muthu says.

"Not a good choice," the woman says. "The lump sum will be much lower."

"We don't want that one," Muthu says.

"It shouldn't even be an option," the woman adds. "We want you to maximize your returns."

"We have a big garden now," Latha says.

"I suppose it is a compromise," the woman says, her eyes locked on Latha's. "You get something, you lose something." She seems irritated, Latha thinks, and the irritation makes her look ugly, pinched, boyish.

"We understand," Muthu says. He taps the layout he likes with his pen and smiles at Latha. "We are looking forward to our new flat."

"Has this house always been in the family?" the woman asks Latha, and her tone becomes softer, as if she suddenly cares. "I grew up near the hockey stadium. I used to walk down this street on my way to school."

"I am not from Bangalore," Latha says. "We inherited this house from his aunt."

"But you have the attachment," she says. "I can tell." She tucks a loose strand of hair behind her ear and smiles at Latha. She has switched to Tamil, using the formal *you* to show respect, yet Latha can tell that there is a lack of it.

"Most women are eager for a new kitchen and nice bathrooms. My mother included," the developer continues, as if she herself is not a woman. "Did you raise your children here? I have two. A boy and a girl. Nine and ten."

"We have two," Latha says. For a moment, she feels more accomplished than the developer, since her children are already grown. "Also a boy and a girl. They want us to take the deal."

Most of Latha and Muthu's neighbors on Model House Road have already taken a deal. Some signed on with developers years ago, and were already living in comfortable modern flats. Latha visited one of them. It was nice—the tile floors looked easy to clean, as did the granite kitchen counters. There were outlets everywhere, and windows with mesh to keep the mosquitoes out. There were showers with decent water pressure, and a raised divider between the toilet and the shower to prevent the entire bathroom from getting wet.

None of this had been enough to convince Latha. She was accustomed to No. 16 and its minor inconveniences, even the tuft of yellow mold that grows under the kitchen faucet, which she scrapes off every three weeks with a spoon. Even the large crack that runs from one end of the hall to the other, through which a long line of black ants emerges, making their daily pilgrimage towards the kitchen—it gives her satisfaction to douse the ants with a thick coating of green Dettol, and wipe them up with a rag.

The woman uncrosses her legs and turns her attention back to Muthu.

"I do not wish to rush you, but we need a memorandum of understanding so I can draw up the paperwork," she says. "Before GST starts."

The Goods and Services Tax, also known as GST, had recently passed and would go into effect in thirty days.

"No more projects after that?" Muthu asks. His hands are in loose fists, rubbing against each other, a sign that he is worried.

The woman shakes her head. "An eighteen percent tax is too much. No new flats for a while. It is bad news for everyone. When we start again, the flats will be smaller. The lump sum will be less."

"We can make our decision today," Muthu says quickly. "Right?" he says to Latha. "We can even sign right now."

"We need more time," Latha says.

"We have a layout we like," Muthu says.

"I can come back in the evening, if you need to discuss it," the woman says as she stands up. "But that will be your last chance."

Once again, she looks at Muthu when she speaks, as if Latha is no longer there. Latha decides the company did not send the woman to convince her, but to entice Muthu. The woman hands Muthu a business card. "I have one more appointment on your street, so I must excuse myself."

It must be with Old Mr. Ravi, Latha thinks, though she knows the long-retired, widowed high court judge despises the developers even more than she does. He is the only other resident of Model House Road who still lives in his original home.

The woman picks up her leather tote and walks to the door. Latha watches her put on open-toe sandals with heels, so impractical for the unpaved stretches of Model House Road.

After the woman leaves, Muthu picks up the papers she left behind. He has the same large, thick hands he had thirty years ago, when the priest instructed Latha to take his hand and walk around the holy fire during their wedding ceremony in Chennai.

The morning after their wedding, she and Muthu took

the Lalbagh Express to Bangalore. That was when she first saw the custard apple tree and Binny, who sat on the bench next to the tree waiting for them. Binny was Muthu's aunt by marriage, a widow. Muthu had come to live with Binny and his uncle at No. 16 Model House Road when he moved to Bangalore for college. They had no children of their own, and offered him their spare room. He never left. They treated him like a surrogate son, and he soon realized that if he stayed around long enough, he might inherit the house.

Now Latha turns and walks through the doorway that leads into the hall.

"The timing is good for me. For us," Muthu says. He trails her into the kitchen. "We can sign this evening, can't we?"

He is a certified public accountant but has never done accounting work. He has spent his career as a mid-level cog at the Water Supply and Sewerage Board, supervising a dozen laborers and reporting to a line of five bosses, including the chairman of the agency. It is a reliable government job, with steady pay and the guarantee of a solid pension after retirement. In fact, it was his job that had appealed to Latha's parents when they were looking for a husband for her, even though he grew up in Karnataka and spoke Tamil with a Kannada accent. Latha's prettier twin sister had married into a wealthier family, right in Chennai. "At least he is stable," her father had said to the marriage broker about Muthu. "For Latha, I think that will do."

Soon, Muthu will start collecting his pension. Sixty is the mandatory retirement age, and his birthday is only three months away. As freedom approaches Latha observes that he walks with a lightness, a bounce to his step that he previously did not have. Of this, she is envious. After their daughter, Deepa, was born, Latha took care of the baby and the house. When Deepa was five, their son, Shiv, was born, and the work of caring for an infant started anew. Then Binny fell gravely ill, and Latha nursed her for two years, until she passed away. Eventually Muthu's widowed mother came to live with them, and Latha took care of her, too. Though her children are grown, soon there will be a grandchild, dropped off daily. Deepa, who is currently pregnant, works for an American company called Accenture. Deepa's salary is high but her hours are long and unpredictable. Latha's job, if it can be called that, does not appear to come with the benefits of retirement.

"What are you thinking?" Muthu asks her. He is eating a piece of custard apple, plucked from the tree in front of their house. He puts a seed in her mouth, and she sucks the white, creamy, velvety flesh off it, inhaling its sweet aroma. She cannot tell him the truth, that she is thinking about him, comparing her life to his. He would not understand. In his mind, she knows, their lives are not separate. They had one life, and they had lived it together.

"The house," she says.

She opens her mouth for another piece of apple. The fruit is ripe, and its juice spills over her tongue.

She knows he wants to take the money from the development company and travel for a year. He wants to go to Ooty and take a boat ride, climb a hill and feel the cool Nilgiri air blow on his face while they share a box of strawberries. She knows he still feels guilty about canceling the Ooty trip they were supposed to take after their wedding, and there are other places he wants to see now, too. The coffee estates in Coorg. Palaces in Rajasthan. He wants a picture of himself riding on a camel in the Thar Desert. They are not well-traveled people, having never ventured beyond the old temples within driving distance of Bangalore and Chennai. "I want to spend time with you," he often says. "And see the country before we grow too old."

She was not opposed to this, not exactly, but the thought of leaving home for a full year and coming back to a completely new flat—modern but gardenless—left her feeling deflated.

"I am looking forward to finally getting this settled today," Muthu says. "I am adding Panchgani to our tour. I read about the waterfalls in the paper yesterday."

"What about the children?"

"Shiv is working. We can visit him in Delhi. Deepa is married and working."

"The baby?"

"She can hire a nanny. These days it is what people do," he said. "And her mother-in-law will help."

"Sixteen others will be living here," Latha says. "Once we rebuild." She takes a plastic cutting board out of the dish rack, its surface stained by the juices of vegetables over the years. "Imagine, all on this one plot."

She peels the papery skin off a small red onion, and begins to chops it into tiny pieces. She blinks away her tears.

"Let me help you," he says. "Don't cry."

She does not laugh at his joke but lets him take over the chopping while she begins washing the vegetables she will cook today: small round potatoes, slender purple brinjal, and elongated, lantern-like okra. It is Friday, so there will be chicken curry, too.

Muthu never used to help her cook, but as his retirement approaches, he seems eager to assist.

She uses a second cutting board and another knife to cube the eggplant, dropping each piece into a bowl of salted water so it does not turn brown.

"How would Binny feel about us turning this house into a tower of flats?" she asks him. She keeps her eyes towards her chopping and braces herself for his response.

"We owe her nothing," he says. "Binny is dead."

"Ssshh."

Using *that* word, instead of *gone*, it was so callous. As

long as No. 16 stood, Binny lived in it. Latha could feel her presence.

Binny's real name was longer, an unusual name that Latha can never quite remember. Nobody had liked it, not even her parents, so she became Binny. There was never an honorific attached—no Binny Akka, or Binny Mami, or Binny Athai—just Binny, to children and adults alike. That first day when Latha arrived in Bangalore, she bent down to touch Binny's feet, but Binny pulled her up by the shoulders, held on to her, and looked her in the eyes.

"None of those formalities in our house," she said. "This is *our* house now."

Latha stared back and took her first long look at Binny. She was not fair-skinned, nor was she beautiful. Her front teeth stuck out over her lips when she smiled. Her eyes were small, her cheekbones not high enough to have ever attracted much attention. But for an older woman, her cheeks themselves were plump, subtly dotted with sunspots. The whites of her eyes were white, free of the red veins that had already crept into Latha's parents' eyes by then. She looked carefree.

"You have asked me so many times," Muthu says, interrupting Latha's memories, his voice too loud. "And I have told you. The house belongs to us. This is our house."

Latha loses her breath when he says *our house*. She puts down the knife and leaves a piece of eggplant to darken on the cutting board. She walks to the hall and sits on the love seat.

Muthu follows her out.

"What is it?" he asks worriedly. "Are you okay?"

"Yes," she says.

"Do you need water?"

"No." He had managed all their affairs for so many years. Their bills. Their bank accounts. Their taxes. Everything. She just signed off when he needed her to.

"I brought you some anyway," he says. He hands her a stainless-steel tumbler filled with water. "Have it."

Her face feels flush and the tumbler is cool to the touch. She presses it to her cheek and then takes a sip. "Yes," she says. "This is our house. That is exactly what I was thinking."

Muthu sits down next to her, kisses her cheek, rubs her back and sings. "My Fair Lady, my fair lady, one a penny, two a penny, my fair lady." He often serenaded her with this blending of two nursery rhymes when the children were young. It made Deepa and Shiv laugh and laugh.

"Stop," Latha says. "Stop."

She walks back to the kitchen. She fires up the gas stove with the butane lighter and waits for the cast-iron pan to get hot. Then she pours two spoons of oil into the pan, and adds in a pinch of mustard seeds and a handful of curry leaves. When the seeds sputter, Muthu wordlessly hands her the stainless-steel bowl filled with chopped onions and she adds them in.

"I do not want us to make a rash decision," she says.

"All I meant was Binny would want whatever is best for us," Muthu says in a calm voice. "She would not want us to make a decision for *her*." He fills the onion bowl with water from the sink tap, but Latha tells him to leave it. "Servant lady will be here soon," she says. "Why bother?"

He turns her from the stove, and bends slightly at the knees to kiss her in the dip between her collarbone and neck. First on one side, then the other. His mustache hairs tickle her and she laughs and pulls away. He leans forward and kisses his way up to her lips, standing up straight as he does so. She relents and presses her lips back against his. She can smell the Pears soap on his skin.

"Is there time?" he asks.

Latha turns her back to him and shakes her head.

He sighs. "I need to go to the office, then," he says. "See you in the evening."

"I have not made my decision yet," she says, though he has already left the kitchen.

After she finishes cooking everything but the chicken curry, she goes outside to take care of the plants. She waters the tree, picks two more custard apples, and then walks through the house, taking the metal can with her so she can water the plants in the back.

Binny had planted everything in the garden. The custard apple tree, the curry leaf, the mint, and the coriander, all in large pots in the back. She taught Latha how to harvest the curry leaves for cooking.

"Only take the big, dark ones. And chop them up when you cook. Your hair will stay black and thick if you eat them."

Upstairs, on the rooftop, there is a jasmine vine growing in a long, rectangular clay pot. Latha carries a full can of water upstairs, along with crushed eggshells and the morning's coffee grounds. She inhales. The jasmine flowers in Bangalore were smaller and stubbier than what Latha grew up with in Chennai, but the blooms were still fragrant.

"Sprinkle the shells and grounds right around the plant, like this."

From the rooftop, Latha can see all of Model House Road. Originally, all the homes on Model House were identical. They were simple, practical homes, functional and flat-roofed, nothing like the Gothic bungalows with triangular gables on Alexandra Street, or the large homes on Richmond Road with powerful columns and arches. Built by the government in the late 1940s, the homes on Model House were distributed to high-performing, mid-level civil servants a few years before the last British troops left India. Binny's father was among the lucky few to get one. The houses had been passed on to children or grandchildren, who otherwise could never have afforded property in central Bangalore.

The houses were basic, with concrete floors stained with red oxide, two small bedrooms, an indoor and outdoor bathroom, a compact kitchen, and a hall with just enough space for two couches, a TV, and a small dining table. Families made changes over the years, adding Western toilets, kitchen cabinetry, multispeed ceiling fans, and in the case of No. 16, built-in wardrobes selected by Latha. But from the outside, the houses looked the same for decades. No. 16 was distinguishable only because of its custard apple tree.

Now, except for No. 16 and Old Mr. Ravi's house, all the plots have been converted into flats. Within the gates of the plots, Latha can see motorcycles, scooters, cars, and bicycles. So many people where there had once only been a family of four or six. The street is getting too loud these days, and polluted, she thinks. Too many horns. Too many rickshaws, picking up and dropping off visitors and schoolchildren. Even taking a short walk is suffocating.

They could move away, sell the property to developers and buy something in the outskirts of the city. Three crores they had been offered, after all. And that was two years ago. They could probably get more now. With half that money they could buy a plot of land with an entire coconut grove behind it. She could have a garden ten times the size of her current one. And there would be money left over. They could travel, maybe even go abroad, to Singapore or Malaysia. She could buy loads of presents for her grandbaby. But even as she has the fantasy, she knows it is not what she wants. Model House Road is a memory box of her life. A tiring life, but still her life. She picks a handful of jasmine blooms, bring them to her nose, and inhales—she has always found the scent both irresistible and cloying—and walks down the steps, back into the house.

At a quarter to eleven, the servant woman arrives to wash the dishes, and to mop and sweep the floors. She is a short, dark woman, muscular at the arms and lean at the stomach.

"How are you?" Latha asks, though she does not want to know.

"Why do you even ask?" the servant woman says. She tucks the end of her sari pallu in at her waist and knots her braid into a bun before turning on the tap. "Life goes on."

"All of our lives go on," Latha says.

Latha hurriedly pours herself a glass of milk from the pot on the stove, worried that if she does not leave the kitchen quickly the woman will trap her into a conversation. To the milk, she adds a spoon of Haldiram's rose syrup, bright pink and sticky, and stirs it vigorously. Then she adds in a half spoon of sugar and stirs again.

"Scrub the dishes properly today, will you?" Latha says to the servant. "Yesterday, I found dried sambar sticking to the edges of the pot."

Latha goes out back and sits on the rattan easy chair by the potted plants. She allows herself this rose milk break every day, both because she enjoys the sweet, frothy drink, and to keep away from the servant woman, who speaks too frequently of her alcoholic husband who has cancer. The disease, the servant woman likes to say, "spreads like a vine." Latha is empathetic but weary. She believes that the woman's husband has cancer, but wonders how he has managed to keep drinking so much through the ordeal.

Latha looks at her phone. One of Muthu's cousins who lives in Albuquerque, New Mexico, has been digitizing family photos and sending them to everyone on WhatsApp. Today, Latha receives one. It is of herself, with Binny, laughing, sitting behind the house exactly where Latha is right now. Binny on the rattan chair, Latha on the step beside her. She looks at the photo more closely and realizes that she is the only one laughing in the photo. Binny's hands are in the air and she looks like she's having fun, but she is not laughing. She is talking, surely saying something that Latha finds amusing.

"You and Binny. 1997. Looking happy. Not long before her death," Muthu's cousin writes.

"What should I do, Binny?" Latha says out loud.

Her phone rings. The photo disappears from her screen, and Muthu's mustached image appears.

"How are you feeling?" he asks. "I was so worried this morning."

"It was nothing," she says, annoyed that he is calling during her break. He should know better. "I am perfectly fine."

After the servant woman leaves, Latha inspects the pots, pleased that after the scolding they seem to have been scrubbed vigorously. Latha has a quick lunch and then empties the clothes from the washing machine into a blue plastic bucket, and hangs them up to dry in the back. She makes the chicken curry. It is Binny's recipe that she follows, not her mother's, because that is the one Muthu likes. She uses the mixie to blend raw ginger, garlic, and onion into a paste and then cooks the paste in a pan on low heat, taking extra care not to let anything burn. To this, she adds chopped tomatoes and cubed pieces of chicken thighs. Regardless of what happened in the morning, she wants Muthu to at least enjoy the chicken.

Binny also taught Latha how to cook the specialties of Karnataka, things Muthu loved but Latha had never heard of before moving to Bangalore. Flatbread made of sorghum flour, cucumber dosas, and bisi bele baath made with freshly ground coriander, cumin, and fenugreek seeds. When she cooked, Binny liked to tune into Radio Ceylon and sing along to film songs.

"Dance with me," Binny said one day, when a jazzy number from the latest hit Tamil film came on.

As the music played, Binny threw her hands up, ladle still in one hand, and slid across the kitchen floor into the dining area, pretending to be the actress in the movie.

"Dance!" she insisted.

Latha tried, but her arms felt floppy, her legs stiff.

"She went to my school," Latha said. "This actress."

"She must be so dramatic, something special."

"No different from the rest of us."

Binny smiled at this, and handed Latha a cloth to wipe the counter.

"That says more about you than her," Binny said. "There. The bisi bele baath is ready. We just need to add roasted peanuts and chopped cilantro. We can enjoy the rest of the afternoon. Where shall we go? What shall we do? A matinee? Ulsoor Lake?"

They went to Cubbon Park that day, and rode on the children's train that went around the park. Latha was embarrassed to be on the ride without a child, but Binny yelped with glee, either unaware or unconcerned that others were watching. Afterwards, Binny bought two tall glasses of fresh sugarcane juice from the stand by the children's train.

"Drink, no?" she said. She gulped the juice, and gestured towards Latha to do the same.

"There are so many flies on the press," Latha said.

"If we get sick tomorrow, we will worry about it then."

Then she took Latha to Commercial Street, where hundreds of tiny shops were packed on either side of the single narrow road. She pointed to a shop selling Kashmiri shawls. "I'd buy you that red one," she whispered. "But then he would find out we were here."

Another day, they went to M. G. Road and ate vegetable sandwiches at Koshy's, and drank filter coffee at India Coffeehouse. They never told Muthu about the excursions.

"Absolutely no need," Binny said.

On one occasion, Binny even arranged for Latha to travel to Chennai alone, to attend a cousin's wedding. Muthu had said he was too busy to drop her off, so Binny put Latha on the morning train after he left for work. Latha, after having a delightful time at the wedding, returned to Bangalore by the night train. A red-faced Muthu met her at the station, and snatched her travel bag from her hands.

The fun with Binny lasted two years, until Latha became pregnant with Deepa. Once there was a baby, there was no time, and Muthu's eyes grew more watchful, even more protective than before. After Deepa, there was Shiv, and then Binny fell ill.

•

At three o'clock, Latha goes for her daily walk. She considers going beyond Model House Road today. She could, if she wanted to. Nobody was there to stop her, just like nobody had stopped Binny. But Latha decides against it. There is no need. Two times up and down the road was enough. Her doctor said she was healthy for her age.

On the walk, she meets Old Mr. Ravi. The grumpy widower has fluffy white eyebrows and no hair, and though he is sound of mind, he walks around the neighborhood in his black gown as if he is about to speak in court. He is eighty or so, as Binny would be if she were alive. Like Binny, Mr. Ravi had moved to Model House Road as a child.

"How are you?" Mr. Ravi asks Latha. He uses a cane to walk. "Are they still after you?"

"Yes," Latha says. Then she surprises herself by saying, "This time, we are doing it."

"Our houses are all we have."

"But new plumbing. Modern interiors. Are you not tempted? All at no cost."

"No cost," he says in his scratchy voice. He shakes his head. "No cost?"

Then he walks on, faster than usual, as if Latha's words have attacked him.

She heads home, looking into the windows of the flats she passes. She admits to herself that she wants the new kitchen, and the new bathroom, and the nice finishes. She could live without the mold and ants. She pauses in front of Mr. Ravi's house. The walls are dirty. Much of the green paint has flaked off, and the house has a sorry, terminally ill look to it. There are shingles missing from the roof. During monsoon season, surely there were leaks.

Back in No. 16, Latha sits on the bed in Binny's room. They kept calling it Binny's room, and Binny's bed, even after it became Deepa's room, and Deepa's bed. At the very end Binny spent long hours in the bed, reading short stories in old copies of *Kumudam*, her favorite pages creased with tiny triangles at the corners. Visitors dropped by with sweets and books, stayed a short while, and left. Latha attended to them, serving snacks and tea or coffee. But most of the time, while the kids were in school and Muthu was at work, she and Binny were alone.

"Because you're here, I don't need to be," Binny said to Latha one day, as she lay in bed. Latha was pressing her calves. "You cannot imagine my relief."

"You mean to take care of Muthu and the kids?" Latha asked.

"No," Binny said. "For the house. I left the house to you. You mustn't tell Muthu."

"You are joking," Latha said. She stopped pressing Binny's legs. "This house?"

"The only one I have. You think I cannot see what your husband is up to? Binny this. Binny that. He has had his eye on this house since he moved in."

"But what is mine is his," Latha said. She started pressing Binny's calves again. "How does it matter?"

Binny laughed.

"You may not think it matters now, but it will. Save it and use it when you need to," she said. Then she commanded, "That's enough. You rest."

When Binny died and Latha and Muthu read the will together, he was shocked and she feigned shock. For a few days, he was sullen. Then, over breakfast one morning, he said, "I suppose it does not matter. We are as one."

And indeed, it had not mattered. For twenty years, they had not spoken of it. For twenty years, it had been forgotten.

When Muthu gets home from the office, Latha is sitting on the cane love seat, watching a Tamil serial, folding the laundry. She mutes it, but turns on the subtitles so she can continue to follow along.

"The developer will be here soon to collect the paperwork," Muthu says. He holds up a small cardboard box with twine around it. "I brought malai sondesh from K. C. Das so we can celebrate!"

"If you bring the plans to me, I will show you what I decided," Latha says calmly. She keeps folding the clothes.

"Show me? What is wrong with you?" He seems amused. He goes to the TV cabinet and opens the drawer where he put the papers that morning. He hands her the floor plan he likes. She does not take it.

"Not this one?"

"No."

"This one?" He tries to hand her another.

She wills herself to hold her body still, to keep breathing in and out. She shakes her head.

She raises her right hand and points to the plan with the smallest square footage. The one that preserves the tree. The one with the L-shaped garden.

"I know you love the garden," Muthu says sweetly. "But it is no bigger than our house now. You know that."

"It will have the upgrades we need," she says.

"Come on, let's take care of this and enjoy our sweets."

"I have decided."

"Ridiculous," he says. He had been leaning on his left foot, but she sees him shift and plant both feet firmly on the ground. "Think about what you are saying."

"I have."

"Latha," he says.

He looks at her. She looks at him. She sees the recognition in his eyes. She could be happy with that. Just that.

But this is her house. This one time, she has power. She feels something wicked zip through her body. It is a feeling Muthu must have had for years. Not in his workplace, where he was a cog. But at home, with her and Deepa and Shiv.

This was what Binny had meant. It was not about the house, it was about the *feeling* that owning the house gave Binny. The same winning feeling, Latha thinks, that the developer woman must have each time she makes a deal. The jolt of strength that Deepa feels at Accenture, when she is supervising a project. This is Latha's chance to know this feeling, to quietly hold it close.

"Are you really going to do this?" Muthu asks.

It occurs to Latha that Muthu's choice is truly the better one. They do not need a large garden. A small one would be fine. A larger flat is better for when the kids visit. For when they have grandchildren. The bigger lump sum would let them travel in luxury. She wants that. She wants to travel. She considers changing her mind, compromising. But she also wants the custard apple tree. She wants the plants in the back. A place to drink rose milk. Even if it means choosing impractically.

"I am sure," she says.

"Disgusting."

Muthu lets out a wordless shout, as if he is in physical pain.

"I'm going for a walk around the lake. You sign the papers yourself."

"I made Binny's chicken curry for you," Latha says, as he turns to leave the house. She swallows. "It turned out well."

"I cannot stop you from doing this," he says, pausing in the doorway. "But do not expect me to be happy. Enjoy the sweets."

She had thought it would break her. That she would collapse. But the moment he leaves, her shoulders drop, a tension is released, and there are soft, silent tears. She reaches for the end of her sari's pallu and wipes away the wetness. Then she exhales into the cloth. The heat of her own breath warms her face.

When the developer woman arrives, Latha tells her which plan she has selected.

"Are you sure? Should we wait for your husband? I know I said today, but I can come tomorrow."

"Two signatures of mine are all you need, yes?"

Latha signs carefully, in neat block letters, her pen pressing hard against the paper on the glass table. The box of sondesh sits on the table between them, unopened. The first time Latha signs, her hand wavers a bit, but her second signature is steady and sure.

Three Trips

I.

For months before my first trip to India, Mom collected gifts for everyone that we would meet. Soft-bristled toothbrushes, bars of soap, and BIC pens that said "Made in America." We went to Monroeville Mall every weekend. Radio Shack was giving away free beach balls, and we collected ten of them, one for every cousin, before the salespeople caught on. Mom bought cardboard canisters of Tang and Pringles, jars of peanut butter, packets of almonds, and bags of Hershey's Miniatures. Slowly, our two-bedroom apartment in Pittsburgh filled up. Our closets burst with American paraphernalia.

Mom accounted for everyone: the children, the elderly, the neighbors, the maids, Chithappa's receptionist, even Aunty's sister, whom she'd never met. She wanted everyone to have a tiny piece of America. This was 1990, and I was nine years old. Though I was eager to travel, and to meet my cousin Padma, the gifts were perplexing. Why would someone want a pen, a bar of soap, a toothbrush?

"Because it's from America," Mom said. "Because it's different. Because it's better."

For Aunty, we bought a shiny department-store watch made of braided metal, with rhinestones. For the baby she was pregnant with, we bought a yellow romper and a onesie that said "Little Peanut." For Chithappa and Grandfather, there were disposable razors and white cotton undershirts.

For Padma, I picked out a white dress made of organza with a red satin sash around the waist. I ran my fingers through the layered petticoat. It reminded me of what Julie Andrews wore in *Mary Poppins*, my favorite movie. It was a dress that I myself would have loved to have.

"It will get dirty in India," Mom said doubtfully, when I picked it out at Sears. "But okay."

"She will love it," I said, though I could not possibly have known. We had never met.

Dad drove Mom, two-year-old Divya, and me from Pittsburgh to New York, where he dropped us off at JFK International Airport. He would fly to India a week later, when work permitted. At the gate a large man, eager to change his seat assignment, knocked Divya in the head with his oversized duffel bag. She toppled over.

"Sorry," he said, without stopping to look.

Mom, her mind on boarding passes and passports and cash in two currencies, simply reached her arm down and stood Divya back up. It was I who squatted to the ground to comfort my sister, despite my lukewarm feelings towards her. I offered her a tiny colored candy from the stash in the front zip of my backpack.

"Don't cry," I said. "Soon we'll be with Padma."

"Pad-ma," she said.

"She's our sister," I said, repeating what Mom often said to me.

Also in my backpack was the white dress. Mom had put it in one of our large suitcases along with the other presents, but I had retrieved it.

"I want to keep it safe," I said. Every so often, I checked on it.

I must have slept through most of the final leg of our journey, because before I knew it, we were at Madras Airport, searching for Chithappa. He was waiting just beyond the metal gate, among hundreds of others frantically waving to loved ones. I immediately saw a resemblance to Dad, in the way that he moved. I saw it in the way he bent to pick Divya up, with his right knee down and his left knee up. I saw it at the edges of his smile, in the way his lower lip popped slightly above his upper one. When he patted my head and then my cheek, I could smell the cool, fresh fragrance of his soap and wondered whether he washed his hands often because he was a dentist. Divya did not cry in his arms. Perhaps she saw the resemblance too, or felt it. Like Dad, Chithappa was tall and muscular. Both of them were athletes when they were younger. Chithappa was a basketball player, Dad a track star. They both had thick black hair. Chithappa had a dirt-colored birthmark on his right cheek. Divya reached out and touched it.

"Shall we go?" Chithappa asked me. "Padma is at home, and she cannot wait to play with you."

He drove us to the house in his five-seater, a Maruti 1000. He had bought it just one month ago, he told us proudly. It was a bumpy, jolty ride, for two thrilling hours over unpaved roads. I sat in the back in awe, free of a seat belt, and aware for the first time that there existed a world of people that looked like me. The pigtailed schoolgirls in their white-and-blue uniforms had sun-bronzed skin and held hands as they walked. I wondered what Padma would be like.

Mom and Chithappa spoke in short conversations that felt unfinished, always using the formal *neengo* with one another, as if they were strangers.

"How is Ramya feeling?" Mom asked.

"This pregnancy is better than the last."

They went through each relative, close and distant, in the same way. Mom never pressed for anything but basic information. Chithappa never offered more. How is Uncle's health. How is Savitri's college. Did Puneet find a job yet.

As we left the city farther behind, there were fewer cars and more buses and scooters. Cows with painted horns held up the traffic. A family of wild boars, led by their dark-snouted mother, trotted by. Chithappa came to a complete stop to let them cross. The car behind him honked and tried to overtake us.

"People here are barbarians," he said. He slammed his hand on the steering wheel, but did not honk his own horn.

When we arrived at the house, Padma was waiting on the front porch. On her forehead there was a small, round red bottu. Her hair was pulled back into two tight braids. Though I had been desperate to see her, in that moment I was overcome with shyness. Behind her stood Aunty, smiling, her cheeks round, her belly a watermelon visible through her flamingo-colored sari. Grandfather stood next to her.

"Go on," Grandfather said to me. "You're sisters." As if it were that easy.

Padma unfurled a woven grass mat on the floor of her bedroom, and we sat on it, side by side. She told me about the horse races Chithappa took her to in Guindy. He was going to win a lot of money there someday, but she was not allowed to talk to Aunty or Grandfather about it. He would win so much that they would be able to move to America, she said. I did not know what a horse race was exactly, but I imagined that it was like the Olympics, for horses. Padma had never seen the Olympics on television.

"What's your favorite My Little Pony?" I asked.

She stared at me, baffled. To cut the awkwardness, I ran to my backpack and got the dress.

"Isn't it beautiful?" I asked. I handed it to Padma.

"I've never seen anything like it," she said.

Later, I gave her a caramel chocolate that I had saved from the airplane, and a bendy, flexible giraffe the flight attendants had handed out to all the children. She bent the giraffe's legs around the softened chocolate. The caramel oozed out onto the giraffe's backside. The result was unmistakable. We laughed until we shrieked, prompting Mom to stick her head into the room and say, "Everything okay?"

"Yes," I replied. "Now go away."

"I have a collection of animals," Padma said. She pulled a metal chest out from under her bed and opened it. Her collection included an elephant, a parrot, a turtle, and a duck with a spring in its neck that allowed it to nod back and forth. The animals were all made of wood and they were unpainted.

She handed me a thumb-sized caterpillar.

"For you."

From then on, we were inseparable. The adults were right. We were sisters.

The day Dad arrived, all of us crammed into Chithappa's five-seater and drove to Madhav's Great Kulfi Shop. Chithappa bought each of us a creamy kulfi popsicle, filled with chopped pistachios. Mom muttered something about the water not being clean, but it was too late. I was licking my popsicle enthusiastically.

"I love it, Chithappa," I said.

"I hear that in America there are ice cream shops with hundreds of flavors," he said. "Is it true?"

"Hundreds," I said. "Come visit."

"Yes, do," Dad said. "A visa will be difficult, though. And there is the cost. But maybe one day. Who knows?"

"Chithappa might win a race," I said.

Padma glared at me.

"I told you not to say anything," she whispered.

On the drive home, Chithappa beeped his horn at people on the streets. Thin, wiry men wearing lungis and women in flowery saris were in deep conversation as he struggled to steer his Maruti through the narrow streets.

"Damn villagers," he said.

When Dad said that we were villagers too, Chithappa laughed.

"Maybe me," he said. "But you, brother, left long ago."

In America, our family referred to "the house" in India, as if it were a single unit. In reality they were two: The houses were connected through an internal hallway, but each side had its own entrance and porch, its own kitchen and bathroom. Padma and her parents lived on one side, clean and organized because of Aunty's efforts. Grandfather lived on the other, with stacks of old issues of *The Hindu*, piles of books and ashtrays on every surface.

Grandfather spent most of his time in his house, and went to Padma's only for meals. I remember his shock of white hair and his eyes, cloudy from cataracts. Though he used a walking stick, his body was muscled, remnants of his training as an officer in the Indian Army. Every morning, he drank milky coffee and ate biscuits on his front porch, delivered by the local canteen. He read the newspaper and checked the obituaries for names of friends. Then he showered and took a long walk around the neighborhood before coming to Padma's house for steaming idlis and hot sambar. In the afternoons, his friends dropped by and they sat on the front porch on rocking chairs, chatting for hours.

Grandfather was kind to Padma and me. When we ran to him, he opened the tin of chocolate crème cookies he kept in his cupboard and handed us two each.

But with our parents, he was stern and distant. Mom tidied up his side of the house and supervised the maid, but like Aunty had discovered long ago, it was an impossible task. The house returned to its messy state almost immediately. Messy, it was at equilibrium. Clean, it was in a state of unrest.

"Leave it," Grandfather said to Mom, when he found her sorting papers in the living room one day.

"There's an electric bill here from five years ago," she said.

"Leave it," he said again, his voice gruff. He pulled the bill out of her hand.

Once, Padma and I went into Grandfather's cupboards in search of crème cookies and found a small album, full of pictures from his days as an army man. There was a black-and-white photo of him in Cairo, with a British officer. He and the other officer had their arms around the bare waist of a belly dancer wearing a sequined bra and silver belts.

We showed it to Aunty, who stared at it for a moment.

"Put it back where you found it," she said.

Instead, we took it to Grandfather.

"My friend Captain James Greene. Good man," he said, squinting at the photo. "Good man. And Egypt was beautiful."

Across the street from the two houses was Chithappa's dental clinic. In Pittsburgh, my father drove forty-five minutes from our apartment in Monroeville to the Alcoa building in New Kensington, where he worked as an engineer. It was a novelty to me that Chithappa had only to walk across the street. Each morning, he saw patients until lunchtime. Then he came home to eat and nap. After his afternoon tea, he returned to the clinic and remained there until late in the evening.

Padma and I often played chess together while sitting on the wide wall that separated Chithappa's clinic from the street. I had brought a travel-size electronic chess set with me from America, something I persuaded Dad to buy on one of our excursions to Radio Shack. As we played, we watched patients go in and out of the clinic, and we tried to guess their dental ailments.

One day, while we sat and played chess, Padma brought up the horse races again.

"You made Amma and Appa fight," she said, her tone even and quiet. "I told you not to talk about it. Please don't do it again."

Every night, my parents, Divya, and I slept on Grandfather's side of the house. Aunty had offered to let us stay on their side, but staying with Grandfather was the right thing to do, my parents said.

The night was the only time my parents had privacy from the rest of the family. Mom and I shared a bed. Dad and Divya slept on the floor, on a mattress that Aunty lent us. Divya fell asleep quickly, but I lay awake for long hours with my eyes closed, fighting the urge to scratch my mosquito bites so that I could eavesdrop unnoticed.

Mom complained to Dad about the uncomfortable

living situation, the strange coldness between Aunty and Chithappa, and Grandfather's impossible messiness. Dad listened patiently, aware that unloading on him was the only way Mom could survive another day in her in-laws' home. She wanted nothing more than to go to our next destination, her parents' place, in a city farther south.

One night, from his mattress on the ground, Dad had something to say.

"Rajan's dental practice is not doing well," he said. "He's been borrowing money from Appa."

"I'm not surprised," Mom said.

Chithappa was drinking too much, too often, Dad said. "Ramya is threatening to leave him."

At this, Mom, whose back was towards Dad, turned around and gasped. I felt the blanket and her warmth pull away from me.

The next night, Dad came back with more stories: Two months ago, Aunty had quietly moved her wedding jewelry to her parents' house. After discovering this, Grandfather had threatened to throw her and her belongings out unless she brought it back.

"It was part of your dowry," Grandfather had told her. "It stays where you stay."

I began to roam the house obsessively while Padma was at school. I had no playmate but Divya, for whom I had little patience, so I listened in on adult conversations, sliding into rooms quietly, pretending to busy myself with pencil and paper.

Once, I heard Dad and Chithappa talking. They were sitting on the wall by the clinic, where Padma and I liked to play chess. Though both of them were tall, their feet did not reach the ground. I found this comical, that two towering men could look like little boys with their feet dangling. I sketched their hanging legs into a notebook.

"Careful about your health," I heard Dad say. "A doctor really shouldn't be such a bad patient."

Chithappa did not put his cigarette out.

Another time, bouncing around the beach ball we gifted to Padma, I went through the entryway that connected Grandfather's house to Padma's, delighted by the ball's response to the hard concrete floors and the high ceilings.

Aunty was at the dining table, cooling hot tea between two stainless-steel tumblers, pouring the long, milky brown strands back and forth. She did this so swiftly that I feared a strand might break and splatter across her pregnant belly and onto the floor. I stopped my ball in action to watch her.

"I will take Padma and leave. This time, I am not joking," I heard her say.

"It's nothing," Chithappa said. "It means nothing."

Chithappa saw me first. "Come, Taruni," he said. "Sit. Aunty will make you Horlicks."

"Why don't you come back when Padma is here," Aunty said. "She has tuition today and will be home late."

Another time, I heard Grandfather talking to Dad, complaining about unpaid loans. They were each holding a section of the newspaper, but not reading it.

"So much drinking," Grandfather said.

"You drink too," Dad said. "You always have."

"I'm an army man. I know how to drink."

"Is there something else he needs help with? Have you asked?"

Grandfather straightened his back and put the newspaper down, looking at my father.

"If you were here, then you might know. You are not here."

When Padma came home from school, the matters of adults were no longer my concern. It was time to play. Together, we drank cups of hot milk mixed with sugar and Horlicks. I thought of telling her what I saw and heard, but having already made a mistake with the horse races, I kept quiet. Most afternoons, we ran around outside and collected rocks. We sat cross-legged on the dirt and made designs with them, stacking some of them and making circles with others.

"Maybe the sprites will visit," she said one day.

It took me a moment.

"Oh, little fairies?" I said.

Then we made stick beds for the toads that came out when it rained.

When we were tired, we went inside and Aunty served us glasses of cold mango juice. Every day, we played chess.

One day, Chithappa took us all to the circus, where we sat in the bleachers and watched midgets juggle, and a family of elephants walk in figure eights. My parents had taken us to a Ringling Brothers show once, but the circus in India seemed more daring. It was less polished and more outrageous.

My father shouted out loud when a clown walked out with three tigers that jumped through hoops.

"Unbelievable," he said disapprovingly.

Slender trapeze artists did flips across a tightrope, their eyes and skin tone more Asiatic than anyone sitting in the audience.

"Cheap labor from Nepal," Chithappa said.

"They look malnourished," Dad said. "And damn unsafe. Does this circus take care of its people."

"Can't you have some fun?" Chithappa said.

"Yes," I said, "it is fun."

Chithappa pinched my cheek.

"Taruni, do you know Chithappa means Small Appa?

Small Father? You want something my brother won't get you, come to me."

"Okay," I said. More clowns marched by. I turned to Padma. "I love the drumrolls." She took my hand in hers.

During intermission, Chithappa bought each of us a newspaper cone filled with spicy peanuts. When Padma dropped her entire cone and started crying, Chithappa bought her another.

"Watch yours, Taruni," Dad said to me. "You won't get another one if it falls."

The next day, while Padma was in school, I jumped rope in the garden. At lunchtime, Aunty asked me to walk across the street to Chithappa's dental clinic and tell him to come home for lunch. He usually came back before lunch, hungry and ready to eat. But that day, he did not materialize.

I waited for a rickshaw to pass, and ran across the street to the clinic.

The front door was ajar. I pushed it open and entered the waiting room. The two rows of benches were empty. The receptionist was not there. The door to the examination room was closed. Inside, I heard movement. A shuffling.

"Chithappa?"

There was silence and then another quick shuffle. The scratch of a chair being pulled out or maybe being pushed in. I opened the examination room door.

This is what I remember: They were both standing. Her sari had orange flowers on it. The armpits of her blouse were damp. Her red bottu was smeared. Her long black braid hung to her waist. Chithappa's blue shirt was buttoned incorrectly and the top three buttons were not fastened at all. This made visible something I had never seen before—a dirt-colored birthmark on his chest, just like the one on his face.

The woman kept her face pointed downwards, but I recognized her. She was the daughter of Grandfather's friend, a schoolteacher who had once given me a notebook and a box of Nataraj colored pencils.

"Taruni," Chithappa said, his voice serious but not stern. "You must knock before entering. Why did you come? Go home."

I ran back to the house, crossing the street without looking both ways. A gang of schoolboys on bicycles almost hit me. They rang their bells furiously.

"Imbecile," one said.

"Crossing the street like a water buffalo," yelled another.

When I reached the house, I ran straight to Grandfather, and he gave me two crème biscuits.

"What happened? You look scared."

I ate the biscuits and fled again, this time to Padma's room, and hid under her bed sheet until she came home from school. "Stomachache," I said, when Aunty asked me why I did not want lunch.

“Poor thing. This is what happens to all foreigners when they come to India.”

She patted me, pulled the sheet up to my neck, and left.

That evening, our last one before we went on to visit Mom’s family, Dad suggested we try a new eatery in town that served pizza.

“My treat,” he said.

“Not a good idea,” Mom said. “Taruni has had stomach pain all day.”

“It’s our last day,” my father said. He waved his hand. “Besides, she looks fine to me.”

The restaurant had too many fluorescent lights. The walls were painted a red-checkered pattern more fitting for a tablecloth. And, in spite of the bright lights, the place felt dingy. The floors were sticky and the booths had torn spots with filthy cotton sticking out. Most disappointing, though, was the pizza itself, composed of buns slathered with ketchup and sprinkled with Amul cheese.

“How do you like it, Taruni?” Chithappa asked.

I did not answer him and instead poked at my food with my finger.

“Your uncle asked you a *question*,” Mom said, clearly irritated by my silence.

“I didn’t like it much either,” Aunty said. “Don’t worry. A little rest and you’ll feel better tomorrow.”

When we returned to the house, Padma brought me the

wooden parrot from her metal chest, wrapped in a handkerchief embroidered with my initials.

"I asked Amma to stitch your whole name on it, but she didn't have time," Padma said.

"I saw a lady in the clinic with Chithappa yesterday," I told her. I couldn't keep it to myself.

"Receptionist Aunty?"

"No," I said. "Colored Pencil Aunty."

"She is a patient," Padma said.

"He wasn't wearing his doctor's coat," I said. "His shirt was unbuttoned."

Padma was staring at me, and it felt like some sort of face-off. I did not know what to make of what I had seen in the clinic, but it was clear to me that it was something strange, something not quite right, something I had to tell her.

"Just don't tell anyone else," she said.

"What about our mothers?" I asked.

"No," she whispered. "I'm just waiting for Appa to win at the races, so we can all come to America. That's his plan. Then you and I will be together."

"My mom says I should tell her everything."

"Well, Amma says all of you have forgotten how to live in India," Padma said. "Who brings a white dress here? How will we keep it clean, with all the dust?"

"I have never lived in India," I said. I could barely utter the words.

II.

For years, my parents were unwilling to buy a plane ticket to go anywhere except India. But the year I turned fourteen, they splurged. We lived, by then, in a simple but comfortable house of our own in a nice suburb of Pittsburgh, with a flat driveway my mother appreciated. Many of our family friends had already done the "California thing," and my parents decided it was time for us to do it too. I claimed I was too old for Disneyland, but when the time came, I packed my suitcase as eagerly as my little sister.

We went to Disneyland first. Our favorite ride was It's a Small World After All, and afterwards Divya and I sang the song over and over as we ate warm, sticky funnel cake dusted with powdered sugar. Another day, we visited Santa Monica and Surfrider Beach. Then Hollywood and, at Dad's insistence, Griffith Observatory, where he was pleased that the clear night sky allowed us to see Jupiter. We drove up the coast towards San Francisco, stopping along the way for fish tacos and horchatas at a seaside joint in Santa Barbara. As I bit into grilled mahi-mahi at the taco place, I thought of Padma.

"Can we visit them?" I asked.

Aunty had not stayed in touch with us after she left Chithappa and moved to California. We knew a few things from our phone calls to Chithappa and Grandfather: Padma was a good student. She played the violin and soccer. Aunty and the kids became United States citizens. My memory of them was from half my short lifetime ago, and I had never even met Padma's little sister. I could not imagine Padma in the body of a teenager, though I was one myself and knew well the awkwardness of all the changes, the curves and sweat and moods. Was she quiet and studious? Fun and outgoing? Forlorn? Long-haired? Thin eyebrows or bushy ones? I had no idea. We'd seen no pictures.

No matter what, I was sure that Padma missed Chithappa. If I were far away from my father, I would miss him. I thought this, even as Dad shook his head at me.

"No, we can't visit them. We have not spoken to them for years."

"She's my sister," I said. "That's what you guys told me."

"Who's your sister?" Divya asked, alarmed.

"Padma is your cousin," Mom said to Divya. "Sometimes we say 'cousin sister.'" Then she turned to me. "Don't call us 'you guys.' We are your parents."

"She lives in California?" Divya asked. "This California? The one we are in?"

"Well," Dad said.

To him, Padma did not live in California. She was as frozen in time to him as she was to me, a little niece who still lived with her father—his flawed but beloved brother—in India, in a home that was not broken. Dad hated Aunty for taking the girls away from Chithappa, for abandoning her husband to rot in his own waste.

"Yes," I said. "She lives in this California."

"Then we should find her," Divya declared.

After a long day that included a ride on a San Francisco trolley car that broke down, a visit to Fisherman's Wharf, and a stroll through Ghirardelli Square, where Divya cried over spilled hot chocolate, my parents argued in the hotel. We were staying at a Holiday Inn close to the airport, where the rates were lower than they were downtown, and continental breakfast was included.

"I don't think it's a good idea," Dad said.

"For whom? You? Him? These children did nothing wrong."

"You are not listening to me."

"This is not for you."

I overheard the whole thing: Mom kept asking. Dad kept saying no. Each time, though, he sounded less resolute.

We drove to Padma's place on our last day in California, a Saturday. That morning in the hotel, Dad opened the small memo pad he kept in his shirt pocket, in which he wrote his contacts. He found Aunty's number. No one picked up, and there was no answering machine.

"Maybe they are traveling," he said, clearly relieved. "Shall we spend the day in Sausalito instead? The guidebook suggests an ice cream shop by the water."

Mom saw my downcast face and said, "We've done enough sightseeing. Let's drive there and knock on the door. Take a chance."

Their place was on Baywood Lane, in Hercules, California. We looked at the large Rand McNally Atlas that Dad had brought with him from Pittsburgh. I measured the distance from our hotel to Hercules with my pinkie nail. It was thirty miles away.

When we reached Hercules, we asked for directions at a gas station. Baywood Lane was a narrow street where the houses were tightly packed. We parked in front of the duplex marked with Padma's address. Across the street were some wild-looking bushes, and behind them, train tracks.

"Trains," Mom said. "Must get loud."

Dad said that he would knock first. But before either of my parents could protest, I got out of the car and followed him.

The girl who opened the door was not immediately recognizable to me, though I knew it must be her. She was wearing jeans and an oversized T-shirt that came down to her knees, and glasses with light red plastic frames. Her hair was pulled into a sloppy high ponytail. She was the same height as me, but a little leaner and her hair was curlier than I remembered. She had a wooden cooking spoon in her hand and I could smell a mixture of ginger, garlic, and onion in the house. It was the same smell that stuck to my clothing after Mom made Indian food.

It was a small place. I could tell just from what was visible over her shoulder. The living room was cramped. There were two identical blue love seats, their covers velvety, and a single fish-patterned armchair. Just beyond the living room, I saw a light oak dining table and four chairs. There was an open textbook on it and a green binder.

"Yes?" Padma said.

"It's me. Periappa," Dad said. "And Taruni. You remember Taruni."

Padma passed the wooden spoon from her right hand to her left. She looked at my father as if she did not know him. But she did. Otherwise, she would have shut that door. I heard small, fast footsteps come through the house and a little girl joined her. Chithappa in miniature, and with pigtails. She even had a small dirt-colored birthmark on her chin.

"My God," Dad said. I could feel the heft of his breath when he said the words.

"Who are they?" the little girl asked.

"Nobody," Padma said. "Go inside and I'll come."

Padma looked at Dad.

"My mother is at work. I am not supposed to open the door while she's gone. You should go now."

"Padma, it's Taruni. Your *sister*," Dad said. "I'm your uncle."

Dad leaned towards Padma, and she took a step back and held the doorknob, as if she might close it on us any second.

"My mother is not here," she said. "And I have only one sister."

She did not shut the door. She just stood there waiting

with that wooden spoon in her hand, watching Dad's discomfort. I could not bear it.

"Let's go," I said. I took his hand. "Let's just go."

We did not speak on the way to the airport. Somehow, even Divya knew to keep quiet. Mom put her hand out for Dad to hold, and eventually he took his right hand off the wheel and put his hand in hers.

"Sorry," I pictured Mom saying later that night, when they were alone in their bedroom, back in Pittsburgh. "I should not have made you do it."

Sorry, I wanted to say.

After we checked in, Dad took us to the Baskin-Robbins at the airport and bought Divya and me ice cream. When Divya dropped her cup on the carpet by the gate, he squatted to the ground, wiped it clean with napkins, and picked her up.

"Never mind," he said. "I'll get you another one."

I sat next to Mom and watched Dad as he stood in line at Baskin-Robbins again, still carrying Divya. I dipped my pink plastic spoon into my ice cream and brought it to my mouth. I kept eating even though I didn't want to. It was cold and sweet and creamy, everything ice cream should be, and yet it tasted like nothing at all.

Mom looked at me and pushed back the loose strands of hair falling over my eyes. She did that often when I was younger, annoyed by my refusal to use barrettes. But now there was no sign of irritation on her face.

"Leave it if you don't like it," she said. "You don't have to eat it."

III.

I saw Chithappa just months before he died, when I made my first solo trip to India, right after college. He had a deep cough and still smoked two packs of cigarettes a day, as evidenced by the ashtrays on his porch, by his bedside, and on the coffee table. Empty bottles of Kingfisher and Johnnie Walker lined the floor in the kitchen. Grandfather had passed away three years earlier, so the other side of the house was dark, empty, and locked up.

I spent an evening with Chithappa. As he closed up the clinic for the night, I asked about Padma. He said that she was fine. They still called him to keep him informed. She would be graduating soon from UCLA, and applying to medical school. I didn't know what to talk to him about, so I told him about my happy memories of her, in excruciating detail. How we collected and laid sticks in the back garden. How we played chess and jumped rope.

He and I sat on the wall outside the clinic, our feet dangling.

"I always thought I was too good for this town," he said. "I wanted to go somewhere better."

He gestured towards the house, just across the street.

"Now I'm the only one here."

He coughed. His arms and legs still looked strong, but his sagging gut mocked that strength. I was concerned for his health, but had no idea how close to death he was.

"I made some mistakes," he said. "Boredom was at fault."

"Everyone makes mistakes."

"Boredom is a thief. It steals our time and leaves us with nothing."

He looked straight ahead as he spoke, right at the house. I understood then that what my uncle had wanted was everything my father had gotten. It was cruel, unfair, for fate to give two brothers such different lives. Chithappa had managed a cheap joyride, but my father had the real adventure.

Chithappa looked at me and gave me a small, sad smile.

A lady selling flowers walked towards the gate.

"Mali, mali, kanagapuram," she said, announcing the varieties she was carrying. Her basket had garlands of white and orange flowers in it, coiled like snakes.

"Buy some for your daughter," she said.

"I will," Chithappa said. He opened the front gate. He held his cigarette in his left hand, and with his right, gave her a ten-rupee note. She snapped a strand off the coil of jasmine and handed it to me.

My hair was short then, so I could not pin the flowers in, but I brought them to my nose and inhaled.

"Padma loved these," I said.

"Did she?" he asked.

I looked at him, at his sorrowful face, and I had an idea. Perhaps it was inspired by Dad, who never told Chithappa about the day we met Padma in California, the day she had humiliated us. "What is the point?" Dad reasoned. It would hurt his brother too much.

"Padma loves buttered bread and hot cups of Horlicks," I said. "Her hair is short like mine." I pointed to my earlobe. "She wears gold studs, just like these. What else would you like to know?"

"Does she read?"

"She loves to read," I said. "She reads outside in the sunshine on Sunday mornings. Twice a week, she goes for long runs, and her favorite subjects are biology and history."

"She loves ice cream," Chithappa said, looking at me, his eyes in search, it seemed, of both the past and the future, even if he knew it was my own invention. In him I saw her and my father both. Maybe in me he saw my father and her.

"She loves ice cream," I repeated.

"Her father misses her," he said.

"She misses her father."

•

For dinner, Chithappa drove me to Star Biryani Hotel, and we ate piles of spicy chicken rice with yogurt. On the way, he played old Hindi love songs in the car. His favorite was from a movie called *Aradhana*.

"Something about the moon, something about the sun?" I asked. I had taken one semester of Hindi in college. "I can't make sense of the rest."

"You are my moon. You are my sun," he said. He looked at me. "It is not a song between lovers. It's a mother singing to a child."

When we returned to his house, we didn't go inside. Instead, we sat on the wall by the clinic until it grew dark and the last of the schoolboys playing outside went in for the night.

Chithappa hummed a Carnatic song. I hummed it along with him. I knew it well. Dad hummed the same song when he read the newspaper in the mornings. He and Chithappa had studied Carnatic music as boys, from a famous singer who gave lessons in exchange for glasses of whisky with Grandfather.

After Chithappa and I finished humming the song, I turned towards him. I was about to speak, but I saw that his eyes were closed, so I kept my thought to myself. *Padma knows this song. She lies in bed with her feet crossed at the ankles, and hums it too.*

Acknowledgments

Heartfelt thanks to—

My teachers: Bret Anthony Johnston, for steadfast support and practical wisdom; Elizabeth McCracken, for care and precision; Michael Adams, for unwavering faith. Paul Harding, Naomi Shihab Nye, and Claire Vaye Watkins.

My wonderful editor, Megha Majumdar, for embracing my work and lifting it up. David McCormick, for believing in short stories.

Classmates, for friendship and guidance, especially Ally Glass-Katz, Leah Hampton, Hannah Kenah, Lucas Loredo, Lara Prescott, and Olga Vilkotskya.

Wah-Ming Chang, Jordan Koluch, John McGhee, Katie Boland, Rachel Fershleiser, Megan Fishmann, Alisha Gorder, Alyson Forbes, Nicole Caputo, Dana Li, Kendall Storey, Laura Berry, Laura Gonzalez, and the rest of the talented, committed team at Catapult.

The Michener Center for Writers, the Keene Prize for Literature, the O. Henry Awards, the Sewanee Writers

Conference, Disquiet International, the Bread Loaf Writers Conference, the Stanford Continuing Studies program, and the magazines that first published these stories, for literary and financial support.

Marla Akin, Holly Doyel, Billy Fatzinger, and James Magnuson. Emily Graff and Anjali Singh. Liz Cullingford, Noreen Cargill, Jen Grotz, Jason Lamb, Adam Latham, Don Lee, Leah Stewart, Gwen Kirby, Jill McCorkle, and Lauren Frances-Sharma. Carolyn Kuebler, Josie Mitchell, Lindsey Alexander, Sara Mang, Jenny Minton Quigley, Meera de Mel, and Jyotsna Sreenivasan. Roohi Choudhary, Sharleen Mondal, Celeste Chan, and Yu-Mei Balasingamchow.

Editors at *The Times*, *The Post*, and *The Sun*, for putting pressure on every written word, especially Frances Stead Sellers, Nancy Kenney, Jim Gorman, Mike Himowitz, Patricia Fanning, and the late David Corcoran.

Lydia Chavez, for telling me to trust my eyes; Sara Houghteling, for nudging me to start and always cheering me on. Jin Auh, for advocacy and encouragement.

My parents, for showing me the world, and for a childhood full of books. My siblings and first and best friends: Shuby, Swathi, and Vignesh. Sid, Sara. Family across oceans and across time. Madhav Bhanoo and the Bhanoo family, near and far.

Naina and Keshav, for reminding me that I was once a child who loved books and dreamed of writing one. And Hemant, always, for a life full of both joy and surprise.

SINDYA BHANOO's fiction has appeared in *Granta*, *New England Review*, *Glimmer Train*, and other publications. She is the recipient of an O. Henry Award, the DISQUIET Prize, an Elizabeth George Foundation grant, and scholarships from the Bread Loaf and Sewanee writers' conferences. A longtime newspaper reporter, she has worked for *The New York Times* and *The Washington Post*. She is a graduate of the Michener Center for Writers, the UC Berkeley Graduate School of Journalism, and Carnegie Mellon University. She lives in Corvallis, Oregon, and teaches at Oregon State University.